SECO

Keno dragged Sheffli_____ pulled him out of the water.

Hook, as he coiled his rope, was curious. "How come you didn't let the son of a bitch drown?"

"I'll never know," Keno said, flinging the half-drowned wolf hunter down on the bank. "It gives a man something to while away them long winter nights just wondering about."

Other *Leisure* books by T. V. Olsen:
STARBUCK'S BRAND
MISSION TO THE WEST
BONNER'S STALLION
BREAK THE YOUNG LAND
THE STALKING MOON
BLOOD OF THE BREED
LAZLO'S STRIKE
WESTWARD THEY RODE
ARROW IN THE SUN
RED IS THE RIVER
THERE WAS A SEASON

KENO

T. V. OLSEN

LEISURE BOOKS NEW YORK CITY

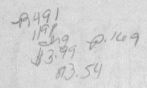

A LEISURE BOOK®

January 1998

Published by special arrangement with
Golden West Literary Agency.

Dorchester Publishing Co., Inc.
276 Fifth Avenue
New York, NY 10001

ISBN 0-8439-4347-5

Printed in the United States of America.

CHAPTER ONE

It was early afternoon when Keno sighted the Mexican. He was about a thousand yards away, staggering along in blind weaving spirals. Finally he dropped on his hands and knees, then slid slowly on his face.

Keno swore dispassionately.

He was feeling pretty snaky to start with. He had been riding this God-forgotten stretch of sand and rock and endless green fog of mesquite for hours since entering the valley from the south. He was tired and irritable with the heat, and hadn't a pleasant thought in his head except the one that centered around a cold bottle of dark Mexican beer. And he was in no damned mood for offering succor to anyone.

He would, though. Keno had learned a long time ago that he was made so he couldn't do otherwise. He'd have done as much for a stray dog as for a man, and probably with better grace.

He reached the Mexican, stepped down off his tall sorrel, and unhooked his canteen. The Mexican was belly-down, feebly frog-kicking while his arms churned in slow drunken strokes, furrowing the hot golden sand with deep angel-wings. Keno stooped and rolled the man over.

He screamed. His body arched in a blind spasm of pain.

No wonder. His naked brown torso was striped with long bloody welts, mostly horizontal, across his back and sides. But his chest looked the worst. Nobody had whipped him there, but someone had held a hot branding iron to the bare flesh for probably the better part of a minute. The skin was blister-raised, seared to an oozing crimson.

Seared with letters: *L. W.*

Blood had trickled down from the whip and brand marks in scabbed dark runnels caked with sand. It had dried in rusty patches on his white cotton trousers. The Mexican's eyelids were so swollen they were slitted nearly shut. The eyes were glazed and didn't register. His tongue, dark and swollen and starting to force its way out between his teeth, had been gnashed to a pulp in the frenzy of thirst.

Keno spilled a little water on the blackening tongue, holding the Mexican's head so the drops would roll down his throat. He took them with a convulsive slobbering. Then he grabbed for the canteen. Keno gave him a little more, and afterward had to wrestle the canteen away from him.

Straightening to his feet then, Keno looked around him. "Christ," he said unhappily.

The valley floor as far as he could see was an intermontaine jumble of fawn-colored flats and swells stippled by the pale green mesquite. It rolled to a dim dragonspine of squashed indigo peaks on the south and west, a closer soar of pine-cloaked mountains on the east, and toward the nearer north a shallow line of hills that looked bare and unpromising.

A few hundred yards away a lone cottonwood nudged up from the sand and mesquite like an anemic sentinel, spreading a scanty shade. For the moment, it seemed as likely a place as any. Keno grabbed the Mexican's wrists, hoisted, ducked, and let the light body collapse across his shoulders. He tramped to his horse and heaved the feebly thrashing man belly-down over the saddle.

Afterward, leading the sorrel, he headed for the solitary tree, noting that the caracoling straggle of the Mexican's prints led away from it. He'd been tied to it: Keno saw the rawhide thongs lashed around the bark-bruised trunk and the blood-soaked loops where the Mexican had finally slipped his wrists free.

By that time, half dead from punishment and from being broiled perhaps for hours by the sun, he had been in no shape to get very far.

Keno found something else in the brush. The carcass of a butchered steer. Was that it, he wondered —a punishment for penny-ante rustling? He had seen men hanged for as much in Texas.

What had been done to this Mexican, though, was worse than hanging. He had been tortured and tied up and left to slowly die. He would have been dead soon if Keno hadn't found him. When the desert turned to a shimmering lake and a man began swimming the sand, he was close to the end.

Stretching his water as far as he could, Keno washed the man's stripes and burns, then laid on some tarry-looking ointment he had obtained in Mexico and had found good for everything from gnat bites to sunburn.

Afterward he wrapped him in a blanket and stayed by him through the afternoon, giving him small draughts of water now and then, sometimes moving him a foot or so, keeping him in the shade.

The Mexican was in delirium. He kept scrabbling at the air with little paddling motions. Finally he ceased the efforts of a tired swimmer and fell into a jerking, fitful sleep. He never stopped groaning and asking for Mariana.

Keno dourly wished, as the dusk drew down like a shabby curtain while he prepared a meager supper, that he knew where the hell Mariana was. Or anybody that could take this unwanted burden off his shoulders.

A hell of a nuisance to be saddled with when he probably wasn't ten miles from Peggott's. But he couldn't find Peggott's or Dad Tasker in this big Godwallow of a valley till he had located someone who could offer directions.

By noon of the following day, the Mexican's baked throat and raw tongue could articulate his painful and pitiful noises into some kind of meaningful speech. Then he didn't want to talk except for *"Mil gracias—mil gracias,"* muttered over and over. He was a gaunt, dried-up weed of a man with a nearly bald dome, a scraggly beard, and terrified eyes that he never took off his saviour.

No blame to him for that reaction. Keno's face was longish and hard-angled, all the softness beaten out of it. His eyes were like mountain water —blue as reflected sky, clear and flat and icy. A knife scar grooved his upper lip on the right side, pulling it to a mild but unerasable sneer. He wasn't big, but he was stocky and compact and had all the quick wiry musculature of a granddaddy rattler.

His *vaquero*'s outfit of brown leather was worn in places to a slick, shiny black. The pants were belled and sideslit at the bottoms, the jacket piped with faded *charro* trim. A black, flat-crowned Spanish hat with a glittering band of conches rode his thick light hair.

"You got anything to say about all this?" Keno asked, not particularly caring whether he did or not.

The Mexican didn't reply. He repeated the question in border Spanish.

The man watched him miserably from the puffy

slits of his eyes. "Your clothes . . . first I thought that you were a Spaniard of the true blood. Those of the old Andalucia—some I saw when I was a boy had such hair and eyes as yours. But you are an Anglo."

"Does this matter, *viejo?*" Keno added in bare explanation, "I have come from living in Sonora."

Again—no answer.

"It was Anglos," he murmured, "who whipped you—who branded you and tied you here—eh?"

The Mexican began to tremble with fear and fever, his teeth chattering. "Please, *señor.*"

"All right, forget it. Who is Mariana?"

Mariana was his wife. *Por favor,* would the *señor* take him to her? *Gracias;* the *señor* was kind. He would direct him to their little house. He had no more to say except that his name was Florentino Deron.

Getting him into saddle was an agonizing business that started several scabbed cuts bleeding again. With Keno leading the animal at a slow walk, they set out roughly eastward and came by midafternoon to Deron's adobe. It stood in a park of pleasant cottonwoods by a sallow trickle of mud-heavy creek whose banks were thickly overgrown with a glossy scrub of willows.

The Derons were very poor. There was only the tiny mud shanty and a rambling pole paddock containing some scrubby sheep. Mariana was at least thirty years younger than her husband, a plump-breasted girl whose eyes showed no relief, only a dark pooling fear when she saw Deron's condition.

Keno helped her get him inside, then asked her for directions to Peggott's. She told him with a trembling haste, and he saw the first break of relief in her eyes when he promptly walked back to his horse—not asking for hospitality, not wanting it.

Not that scared Mexicans in Anglo country were any novelty—the big American landowners always treated the *peónes* like dirt. But the smell of fear

about these two even extending to one who had be-
friended them, was so thick you couldn't cut it.
Keno was as glad to be gone as they were to see him
go....

For the rest of the afternoon he followed the
creek upstream. It was nearly sunset when he came
to Peggott's "hog ranch."

The place was located in the southeast corner of
the valley, tucked between the small hills that
fringed the west boundary of the San Lazaro Reservation. Its patchwork of gray buildings was a dingy
fungus on the green and gold rolls of land. A cluster
of 'dobe hovels as ugly as Deron's squatted between
the frame outsheds and the stream.

It was the usual "hog ranch" that sprawled just
outside any reservation or troop cantonment. Sol-
diers and Indians, trappers and cowboys and
drifters, could get their fill of hogswill whiskey and
venereal women. Keno wasn't particularly fastidi-
ous, but this kind of hole was a little high for his
palate. He felt a dour irritation that Dad Tasker
had chosen it for their rendezvous.

Dad probably had his reasons. He always did.

Keno approached the main house from the side.
He saw a brush corral that held a half-dozen horses.
A man was slogging across the chopped mire of the
yard between the stone-walled well and a horse
trough, carrying a bucket of water in each fist. His
huge soft bulk and his pegleg where a right foot had
been made it a tough chore. Seeing Keno, he came
to a dead stop.

"You Peggott?"

The one-legged man nodded, his eyes lazy and
impervious. He wore a leather apron over a dirty
undershirt. His face was like a bland blob of orange
dough, a toothpick protruding from its tiny slit of
mouth.

"You want supper? A room maybe?"

"I'll stay over tonight anyhow," Keno said.

From one of the 'dobes came a woman's explosive squeal and a burst of Mexican invective, followed by a man's booming laugh. Keno glanced that way, thinking he knew the laugh, then looked back at Peggott.

"Is Dad Tasker here?"

Peggott took the toothpick from his mouth and eyed Keno over more carefully. "Yeah. In the bar. I'll put your horse up. Grain him?"

Keno nodded and dismounted and handed Peggott the reins, afterward heading for the large three-section building that would house a bar and kitchen and other rooms.

Before he reached the door, it opened and a girl came out. She carried a pan of gray dishwater, which she slung out with a snap of her wrist into the muddy yard, spattering Keno's boots.

She wasn't over seventeen and her hair was paler than his, but her eyes were green as a cat's, dark as jade. Her face was deeply tanned, with delicate features. She was already as full-bodied as a woman in her twenties, and her calico rag of a dress clung damply with sweat. Her skirt, like a Mexican girl's, ended at the calves.

She stood curling her bare feet against the hot boards of the porch and watched him with no dare or invitation in her eyes, only a mild curiosity. He guessed that the bold provocation of her body was natural and that she dressed as she did out of necessity.

"Not this way, mister. It's through the kitchen. You go around the other way."

She edged her feet a little apart, emphasizing the fact with her stance. This was her territory. Keno touched his hat and said dryly, "Yes'm," and tramped around the building and onto a long gallery.

He parted the batwing doors and went in. The

barroom stank of the usual ratty odors that such rooms did.

There he was, sitting at a scarred table in the corner. Dad Tasker, the surly old reprobate who had raised Keno. A small man, scarred and gray and bent, with his veined hands crabbed around a tumbler of whiskey. He had probably nursed it half the day: Keno had never seen him drunk. He always put you in mind of a lobo wolf trying without much success to play a hyena.

Keno had taken one step into the room when Dad gave him a slight, barely perceptible shake of his head.

Keno let his glance pass on indifferently as he moved to the plank bar. Dad's signal meant that, for the moment anyway, they didn't know each other.

The reason for that, he supposed, was the raw brute of a man who stood farther down the bar, his fist clamped around a bottle. He as spare but huge-boned with a gauntly hungry face, his hair like moldy straw under a coonskin cap. He wore greasy buckskin breeches and, in spite of the heat, a bearskin coat.

He turned his head and looked Keno over. He took a massive slug from the bottle and dragged a hairy fist over his mouth, still staring. "That's enough spick trim to decorate a Christmas tree."

Keno decided that here was trouble. He didn't really mind. In fact he half-relished the idea of trouble. He was, after all, feeling even more irritable than he had felt yesterday.

"I don't like greasers," the rawboned man said. "Don't like a bastard who gussies up like one."

"I guess that's your hard luck," Keno told him.

The man grunted and emptied his bottle, and banged it down on the bar. *"Peggott!* Where'n hell are you?"

Keno crossed his arms on the bar. He gazed thoughtfully at its scarred top and wondered how long it would take.

CHAPTER TWO

Peggott came in by the back way. Keno heard him pause in the kitchen and say, "Bring me in some coffee, Tally Jo," before he came through the barroom. He wore a dirty carpet slipper on his one foot. The foot and his peg made an old *slap-tonk slap-tonk* sound as he stepped behind the bar.

He reached into a barrel and pulled out a fresh bottle of doctored-looking whiskey. Probably the old rotgut recipe of raw spirits and water. With coloring and peppers and maybe snakeheads.

"Cash."

"Bone Shefflin's credit oughta be worth something," the rawboned man growled.

Peggott chewed his toothpick with that dough-bland look. "Sure it is. You want to hear how much?"

Muttering, Shefflin dug out a double eagle. Peggott changed it to silver dollars from a voluminous pocket in his leather apron and handed Shefflin his bottle and change.

"Tally Jo!" Peggott raised his voice. "You hyper along with that coffee."

"I'm coming. Keep your peg on."

The pale-haired girl entered carrying a tray with

a steaming pot and a single cup, which she set on the bar. Shefflin turned his head again, this time in her direction.

He said, "How 'bout it?"

Tally Jo flicked a cool jade glance at him, her eyes utterly indifferent. "That's what Peg's got the Mex girls out back for. Anyhow you stink worse'n a hog. Why don't you go soak in the crick?"

"Can't abide greasers," Shefflin muttered. He yanked the cork of the rotgut bottle with his teeth. "Men 'r women, I can't stummick them brown bast'rds. I tell you, yesterday—"

But Tally Jo ignored him and went back to the kitchen. Shefflin turned his muddy gaze on Peggott, who was pouring his coffee.

"Like I 'uz saying," Shefflin went on, "yesterday I caught one of them greaser bast'rds from up the valley butchering out one of Mr. Westerman's yearlings. Jesus, did I lay it to that son of a bitch."

"Did you?" Peggott said disinterestedly.

"Sure as hell I did. Tied the son of a bitch to a tree, then doubled up a bran' new rope and laid it acrost his back till my arm like to drop off—"

"Then," Keno cut in very softly, "you branded him. And left him tied that way in the sun."

Shefflin swung half-around, his eyes like murky puddles. He seemed to have trouble focusing them. "Hey?"

"You don't like greasers," Keno said, "so that made as good an excuse as any."

"You the law? Or just a spick lover?"

"I'm the man who found him, that's all," Keno murmured, and now he moved along the bar till he stood less than a yard from Shefflin. The man's rank smell was overpowering.

"You were looking to choose me. Now you can start."

"Why, hell—" Shefflin was blinking rapidly. This was happening too quickly for him.

Keno helped him make up his mind. He gave Shefflin two teeth-jarring clouts with his open hand, flat stinging slaps that were like pistol shots. Then he stepped back and away from the bar, letting his arms hang loose, waiting.

Shefflin rasped a hand over his long, unshaved jaw. Then he gave a roar and lunged at Keno, his arms spread. The man resembled a giant ape in more ways than one. Keno moved out of reach of those great crushing hands, fluidly circling the room. Twice he leaped quickly in and back, fetching the rawboned giant another hard slap each time.

Shefflin was not naturally quick; whiskey had dulled his movements more. He moved carefully, patiently after his lithe adversary, sobering a little more with each open-handed blow that reached his jaw. He began to grin.

Peggott reached down and picked up the sawed-off Greener leaning against a barrel. He eased both hammers back to full cock. He shifted the toothpick to the other corner of his mouth, saying, "You ain't wrecking my place. Take it outside."

Keno glanced at him. "Whatever you say."

Shefflin used the moment to bore in. His fists flailed in great looping swings.

Keno laughed and backwalked out the door. Shefflin followed him, bellowing like a buffalo bull. Out in the open it was far easier to evade the big man's clumsy stalking. Keno was able to keep the flat rays of setting sun in Shefflin's eyes much of the time.

He stayed just out of reach and proceeded systematically, ruthlessly to chop Shefflin down, using his small, hard fists like tackhammers. He delivered blows anywhere and everywhere to Shefflin's big gaunt frame—face, chest, belly, ribs.

It was less of a fight than a slow, calculated butchery. Keno was in no hurry to end it. Shefflin was as immensely slow as his enemy was quick.

Just a matter of staying beyond those big arms or not daring their menace for more than an instant. Or else keeping around to Shefflin's back and punishing his kidneys.

Keno had fought a lot of battles. But he had never enjoyed even one before. This was different. All he had to do was think of Florentino Deron.

Shefflin's face was sliced to a pulped, bleeding mask. He couldn't even touch his lightfooted opponent, and Keno had not missed a blow. Finally Shefflin stopped and yanked a long and wicked Arkansas toothpick from its sheath in his boot.

"That was a mistake," Keno said.

Shefflin sank into the knife fighter's cat-shanked crouch, and suddenly he was more dangerous than he had been, his movements more graceful. This, Keno realized, was Shefflin's weapon.

Keno became more careful, keeping a close eye on that slim nasty sliver of steel. It made dull-glittering arcs and parabolas in the twilight.

Keno watched his chance. Finally he brought up his foot in a lightning kick whose power rippled clear from his hip to his toes. The point of his boot took Shefflin squarely in the wrist. There was a muffled snap of bone.

The dagger's razored steel ripped Keno's leather trousers; the tip broke his skin. That was all.

Shefflin's hoarse scream tore the soft evening air like a ripsaw tearing satin. He fell back, staring at his hand that dangled on a broken wrist.

Keno thought of Deron and beyond him to all of his persecuted race who had suffered at the hands of animals like Shefflin whose claim to superiority was his hairy white skin. He thought of this and of his gentle friends in Mexico, and there was no mercy in him.

He dragged it out for Shefflin, playing a savage tattoo of fists that cut the man gradually to ribbons when he could have ended it any time. Shefflin was weaving in blind, clutching spirals now. Keno wanted him to. Deron had looked this way when Keno had first seen him.

Shefflin was barely on his feet, a bloody shambling wreck, when Keno finally ended it with a short, chopping blow. Shefflin's knees hinged, he folded down loose as a sawdust doll, and his face plowed in the dirt.

Keno swung on his heel, looking swiftly around. He'd been too intent on punishing Shefflin to watch his back, an unusual lapse for him.

Dad Tasker and Peggott were standing on the gallery looking on. Tally Jo was in the doorway, her lip faintly curled in disgust.

A short, powerful, thickset man had just stepped around the corner of the building. Even by daylight his ugly, rocklike features were enough to scare the bejabers out of a body. His red hair was cropped close and flat to his bullet head. A smooth leather jacket was fitted over the stump where his hand had been. A shiny steel hook projected from the jacket.

"How, Keno."

"How, Hook."

Keno wasn't surprised to see Hook Blanding here. He had recognized Hook's great laugh from the 'dobe where the Mexican woman had been cursing.

Hook had attached himself now and then to Dad Tasker's service for as long as Keno could remember. He had been a top cowpoke till he had lost his hand. He still liked punching cows best, but he had been drifting on and off the shady trail a good many years now.

Tally Jo said, "You're bleeding like a stuck pig, mister," and pointed at the dark wetness of Keno's pantsleg where Shefflin's dagger had gone in. He moved his foot and felt the blood squish in his boot.

"Come on in," she said, "I'll fix that."

Dad Tasker gave a surly nod. "Yeah, go 'long. I been waiting around for you weeks, but don't rush none." He moderated his tone then. "We can have supper and talk things out."

Keno glanced at Peggott.

"Peg's all right, kid," Hook said. "Don't mind what he hears."

Peggott grunted and stumped off the porch and bent down to grab Bone Shefflin by the collar. "Gimme a hand, will you, Hook? We'll dunk him in the crick."

Hook clucked his tongue. "Ought to leave the bastard in it then. All right."

Keno followed the girl to the kitchen. He sat on a stool and rolled up his pantsleg while she put on water to heat and ripped up a soft, frayed towel that looked fairly clean.

"Cloth's pretty dear. Hate to waste it this way."

"You don't need to," Keno said reasonably.

"That's for sure. I never see anybody chop someone up like that. You crazy or somewhat?"

"Somewhat." Keno blew on his knuckles. They were skinned and aching, and drops of Shefflin's blood flecked his clothes. He raised his eyes, feeling the sweep of her curious green stare.

"I heard it in the kitchen," she said. "What you said he done to that Mex. That's why I'm doing this."

Keno nodded. "Who's this Shefflin anyhow?"

"He's Major Westerman's wolfer. Puts out poison baits, does odd work around the range, makes do with trapping and hunting and fishing, 'sides collecting bounty and pay for oddments off the Major. Where you get that rig you got on? You been in Mexico?"

"Uh-huh." Keno examined the oozing cut in the knotty muscle of his calf. "Is Peggott your pa?"

"*Him?* Grannies, no." The water was simmering; she poured it into a shallow pan as she talked. "We was from the Ozarks, my paw and me. My ma died when I was little. Paw and me come west a year back. Coming down this valley, Paw took the heaving fits—the bilious or something, I dunno—and died. So I buried him and begin walking. Walked here. Peggott said I could stay on. I just cook his grub and keep his place sightly. Sightly as you can make a sty anyways. Ole Peg, he ain't a bad sort."

Tally Jo knelt on the floor, set the pan down, and began bathing his cut. The hem of her calico skirt had edged up, showing round white knees.

"Seems you know each other, you and that old man Tasker. At first you was making out like you didn't. Course it's none of *my* business. How old're you?"

"Twenty-one, around that," Keno said. "You sure run on a blue streak."

"So would you, you seen nothing but Bone Shefflin's sort day after day. Ole Peg, he never talks. And them Mex girls down in the 'dobes, they don't talk English 'cept for cussing and saying dollars 'stead of pesos. *Dos* dollars. *Tres* dollars." She didn't smile. Her stare was frank and curious. "I suppose you'll be moseying down there. What d'you mean, twenty-one, around that?"

"Means I don't know for sure." Keno paused, then decided there was no harm in telling a few things to a pretty girl. "Dad Tasker found me squalling in the brush back of a saloon one night. This was down by the border. Brownsville. I was two or so. He reckoned one of the crib ladies dumped me there. So he raised me . . . or leastways took me along with him."

"That's real funny." Tally Jo wrinkled her nose thoughtfully. "That Hook—I like him, for all he's ugly as sin. But not that old man you say brought you up. I been watching 'em for weeks now. Mister, that old Tasker is just pure-quill *hard*. I can't see him taking on no foundling."

Keno shrugged. "A man can change. He must of been different then. I don't recollect."

"You didn't stay around with him?"

"Till I was fourteen. He larruped me regular till then. One night I beat hell out of him and run away. I come back after a time and he didn't beat me no more. After that, I come and went as I pleased."

Tally Jo knotted the soft cloth around his leg. A small red stain sprang onto it, but the bleeding seemed to be checked. "That'll do. Heard that Hook call you Keno. Ain't you got no more name'n that?"

"None I know of. Dad busted the table at Keno, night he found me."

"I got a last name." She stood up, holding the pan in her hands with a prideful touch to her stance. "It's Richland."

"That's a fine name." Keno rolled down his pantsleg and rose, giving her a minute bow the way he had once seen a Mex dandy do. "I thank you, madam...."

"Madam! What the hell, you think I got a *place* here?" Angry crimson flooded her face. She looked ready to fling the pan of dirty water at him.

Keno stared at her. Then he started laughing. He couldn't help it. The anger ran out of Tally Jo's look; she even gave a grudging little smile.

"Well, *that* madam, that shines all right. Just that anyone uses the word around *here,* what they mostly mean..." Her small face turned intent and serious. "No wrong in funning 'less a body means wrong by it. I know you didn't. Good thing, too. I don't even hanker being made out a light girl, I tell you. We Richlands was poor, but we got proper raising. And by grab, boy, you better *remember* it."

Keno nodded gravely. "Good thing you told me. I'm a pretty bad sort, you know."

He touched his hat and went out to the back porch to empty the blood out of his boot.

CHAPTER THREE

Keno and Dad and Hook sat around a deal table in the barroom, a bottle and glasses between them. Keno and Hook quietly reminisced about old days, mostly of how Hook had taught Keno what he knew about riding and shooting and hunting. The two of them did justice to the bottle. Peggott *slap-tonked* about the building, lighting lamps as the twilight furred softly into dusk.

Dad Tasker sat with the same drink untouched before him, uninterested in the talk. Keno, while joshing with Hook, kept studying Dad's gray face. It made him think of a wax mask left by the fire till its structure had sagged and collapsed in a ruin of wattles and lines and age-smooth scars. Only a year and a half had passed since he'd last seen Dad, and Keno was surprised at how much older he looked. Otherwise he hadn't changed—as surly and withdrawn as ever, with that same air of nondescript meanness.

Tally Jo began serving the supper they had ordered, carrying the steaming dishes to the table as each was ready. She was in no hurry.

"Goddam it, girl, you jump now!" Dad snapped.

She was carrying a fresh pot of coffee to them,

and she halted, eying him. "You want a hot sham-
poo? Just rough-mouth me again."

Dad didn't answer. Hook laughed quietly. She
slammed the pot down on the table and went back
to the kitchen.

Dad glanced at Keno. "How come you had to bust
up that there Shefflin like you done?"

"You heard him," Keno said. "He tortured a man,
left him to die."

"Yeh," Dad said dourly. "You always was funny
about that kind of thing."

The meal wasn't much. Tally Jo had probably
done as well as anyone could by what was available,
but Keno found little appetite for what she served.
The beef was tough and stringy; the bread made
from flour that should have been thrown out long
ago. The coffee was at least two-thirds chicory.

"Dad, you got a talent for choosing lowdown holes
for powwow. Ain't there a town around here we
could have met?"

"There's a town. But best we ain't seen together
by no law-abiding kinds. I got some strong medicine
to make, boy. Don't want the wrong ears taking it
in."

"So far you ain't said anything." Keno chewed a
jerkylike lump of salty beef, trying to reduce it to a
mouthful of fibers that would slide down his throat.
"I come a long way to hear it."

"Might's well wait till Giles Garfield gets here.
You can hear it all then."

"Who the hell is Giles Garfield?"

"Just a man wants to make a quick pile of
money." Hook hacked on a wrong-way swallow of
coffee. "Dad, you might's well start the telling. Garfield mightn't show up for a good hour or so."

"Just so he shows," Dad growled.

"He will. He ain't missed Tuesday nights with
that little Mex filly yet. Go on."

Dad hunched forward across the table, looking

like a scarred, vicious gnome in the oily flicker of
the lamps. "This ain't like other things we done.
Once you know the what-for, you could cut me out.
So I need your word."

"You got it."

"Well then, ever hear of Major Lewis Westerman?"

"The girl mentioned a Major Westerman. I seen
his initials burned on that Mex's chest too."

"The Major's got his brand on the whole valley,
boy. Owns most of the country you rode over today.
Half a dozen ranches, some mines, 'most all the
businesses in the town of Pecas.

"About a year ago, I guess it was, some fella
working for him stumbled on a big strike of gold
over in the northeast edge of the Major's property.
Leastways he thought it was on the Major's property, so he reported it. But the place was pret' close
to the San Lazaro Reservation line. Close enough so
Westerman had it surveyed. Come to find out, the
strike was just across the line. Means that gold be-
long to the gov'ment.

"Well, that didn't stop Westerman. He set up
cabins by the strike and threw up a big stockade all
around. Hired the best mining men money could get
and a mess of hardcases to guard the place.
Freighted in tons of food and tools."

Hook chuckled. "Ain't that a caution? He's squat-
ting on the government's land and filling his pocket
with the government's gold. The old man sure is got
his gall."

Keno felt a stir of mild interest. "He may be big,
but I never heard of anybody big enough to buck the
federals head-on. Not for long anyhow."

"Hell," Hook snorted. "Suppose'n the government
wants to roust him out. Do that, they got to send the
Army to storm the place. There's only one trail up
and the troops 'ud get chopped to pieces taking it.
Can't get artillery up there. Huh-uh. They ain't

gonna bother less'n someone raises a big whoop'n'squawk. Nobody will."

"Seems the Indians'd make a row."

"Hell, the Utes don't care. Major's tucked his stockade way up on a big stony roost even the devil wouldn't lay claim to."

"That's so," Dad put in, his scarred lips twitching. "Matter fact, though, I doubt the gov'ment ever knows. Major's gone to a sight of trouble to keep the operation quiet. He's skittery, and no wonder. Been working the place since last spring and all through the winter. Got over a quarter million in gold bullion up there...."

"You know a lot for all it's a big secret," Keno observed.

"Coming to that. We—"

Hook raised his one hand, waving them to silence.

They listened. A pair of horsemen were approaching the hog ranch. Boots hit the gallery; two cavalry troopers barged through the door, yelling for Peggott. They didn't even glance at the three seated men. They wanted girls. Peggott appeared, took their money, and led them out to the 'dobes in back.

Dad resumed talking, but in a lower voice. "Reckon we know as much about Westerman's operation as Westerman himself. Giles Garfield is seen to that."

"There's that name again," Keno murmured.

"Good reason, boy. Garfield is engaged to the old man's daughter. Only daughter."

Dad went on. As he explained it, Giles Garfield was a charlatan, con man, and swindler—and had been for half of his twenty-odd years. Somehow, back in New Jersey, he had palmed himself off successfully as the scion of an old English family. For several years he had managed to carry off his precarious and preposterous deception unquestioned, mingling with the best families in the state as an omnipresent houseguest.

Then he had met Luana Westerman, who was at school in the East, while she was weekending at a girl friend's home. Within a month their betrothal was announced. Garfield's parents, of course, sent their blessings from faraway England and regretted that they couldn't convey them in person.

Luana had tried to persuade her new fiancé to return to the West with her. Prospects there were wonderful for young men with talent and energy to invest. By now having thoroughly saturated himself with the lore of the West (as regarded Major Westerman's financial affairs) Garfield had let himself be easily persuaded.

Keno was starting to get the picture. "This Giles Garfield must be quite a bastard."

"A three-ply one all around," Hook grinned.

"I don't care what private ax he's grinding," Dad Tasker snapped. "Main thing, his interest is ours where that gold's concerned. I got my private ax too." His fist squeezed around his coffee cup so tightly that the knuckles whitened. "That's taking a fortune out of Major Lewis B. Westerman's hide."

Keno glanced up from his plate. "A grudge?"

Dad nodded, his eyes glinting. "I had it in for that finehaired bastard a good many years. He done me dirt a man wouldn't do to a dog. I tell you—"

"There," Hook interrupted. "That's Garfield coming. He rides like a six-thumb dude with a sore crotch. Which he is."

Giles Garfield entered. He wore whipcord breeches and a tweedy riding jacket and carried a riding crop. A tall, well-built man in his late twenties, he was handsome in a dark, beetling-browed way. His beard was so heavy it made a black sheen along his jaws, though he'd obviously shaved only hours ago.

He had a deep, strangely sensitive voice with no British accent that Keno could discern.

His hand was large, firm, moist, with that over-broad, too-hearty way of grabbing yours that Keno instinctively disliked. However, he had conceived a dislike of Giles Garfield sight unseen.

Garfield squinted at Keno as if he needed glasses but was too vain to wear them. "So you're Dad's man. Haven't I seen you somewhere?"

"I don't think so," Keno said. "I'd remember a son of a bitch like you."

"What?" Garfield stepped back, astonished. "What's that supposed to infer?" He looked excitedly from Dad to Hook. "What's he mean?"

"Not a thing," Hook said gravely. "Calm down, Giles. Keno's got a funny sense o' humor is all."

"Oh—" Garfield's laughter jarred out in a harsh staccato bray. It startled hell out of Keno; he nearly dropped his coffee.

"Siddown," Dad said gruffly. "Was just telling Keno about Westerman's quarter million in bullion and how he aims to ship it out secret."

"Yes—" Garfield pulled up a chair and sat down between Hook and Keno. "You see, the Major's afraid that if word leaks out, every crook in the country will converge on this bailiwick. So long as the bullion's up in his stockade with guards all around, there's no worry. But once it's on its way East..."

"Major's right or we wouldn't be here," Keno said, a trifle wearily. "Where do I fit in?"

"Ha! Ha!" Garfield brayed. "Very true. Well, I suggested to the Major—I'm engaged to his daughter, you see—"

"I heard," Keno said coldly.

"Yes, well, I suggested that my father's insurance company could handle the job very efficiently. They're used to insuring gold shipments against robbery or loss or acts of God—fire, floods, tornadoes, et cetera. They'll get the gold through safely, maintain strictest secrecy—and if the gold's lost, Major Westerman will be reimbursed. *Now—*"

Garfield tapped an emphatic finger on the table. "The company is sending its two best field agents here. Trusted, experienced men—men I know personally and will vouch for. These two will have complete charge of getting the gold East."

"That's you and Hook, boy," Dad said. He turned a glittering eye on Keno. "You'll be the field agents for his daddy's company. Seeing's there's no real agents and Garfield's real daddy got no company either."

"I'd never have guessed," Keno said.

CHAPTER FOUR

Keno turned his glass slowly in his palm, scowling at it. "Hard to believe this Westerman'd swallow a hunk of bunkum like that."

"Why not?" Garfield's tone was faintly smug. "Part of my cover when I met Luana a full two years ago was that I was in this country seeing to my father's American interests. You see, old chap, my governor not only owns a vast wedge of New York real estate, a Newark law firm, and a New York publishing company—he's a major stockholder in one of the biggest insurance companies in your jolly country."

"I don't see a damned thing," Keno said, "outside of this Westerman could check back and find out quick enough what a damned liar you are."

"But my dear fellow, of course he's checked," Garfield said. He brayed lightly. "Naturally he didn't tell me so—but a man like Westerman would, as soon as he'd learned of Luana's engagement. And when he did, he learned there is a wealthy English family named Garfield—cousins of the British and Continental Rothschilds—who do own the American enterprises I just mentioned. And there's a son and heir named Giles. Met him in a London club several years ago when I was over among our British brethren on—er, another affair. Young rake, but ineffectual. An empty identity that I could fill with any character I chose—on this side of the ocean."

Garfield paused, chuckled "Huh huh," and added, "I can tell you privately that my real name is William R. Lutz and I'm from a little rural village right in New Jersey that nobody ever heard of, called Packpea."

"That's interesting," Keno said. "Tell me something else. How did you meet Dad and Hook?"

"Oh—" Hook winked. "Dad and me was just passing through and laid over here at Peggott's. Giles comes here off and on to see his girlie, and we all got talking. Upshot was, we decided to stay around."

Garfield flushed and smiled. "Yes. Of course I have to be circumspect—wouldn't do for Luana to get wind of my being here. I always speak of business in town—of a vaguely confidential nature. I have to see to my governor's affairs too—means trips back East now and then." A cynical smile touched his lips. "Naturally a man doesn't like to divulge all his personal business. The Major's a man of the world—he understands."

"Well, I'll be a bastard," Keno said. "I guess I'm just too crooked to think of something like that."

"Huh! Huh! Now"—Garfield reached in his pocket and drew out some papers which he laid on the table—"these are your credentials as agents for my father's company. Beautiful job if I do say so—made up by my Chicago pal who forged my insurance papers for Westerman. Also you and I will be old friends. That'll relax any vestige of suspicion."

Keno nodded pleasantly. "Well, I guess it's not Westerman's gold either. Rob a thief to pay a thief, eh?"

"Ha! Ha! Ha! Exactly. You'll do fine, my friend."

Keno murmured, "That's your first mistake," and pushed back his chair and got to his feet. "No dice."

"What!" Garfield stared at him, then at Dad. "I thought you said—"

"He will," Dad crackled. "Damn you, boy, what's sticking in your craw anyhow?"

"A few things," Keno said coldly. "No love lost between us, Dad, but we trust each other. I wouldn't trust this jackass with his own sister. Count me out."

"Wait a minute, dammit! You know me better'n to reckon I'd run in blind. Him"—Dad stabbed a finger at Garfield—"*he's* got to trust *us*. We split the take four ways, and he's got to take our word we'll meet him for the split."

"I don't like the smell of it," Keno said flatly. "If he means to marry this Westerman girl, he's got his fingers in a fortune without raising a hand. Why go to this trouble?"

Garfield had reddened, but he said calmly enough, "Because my time's running out. I'm living under the fact that any day, somehow or other, I could be exposed as an impostor. I've got to get out with what I can. I have more on the table than just a game—I know now that I've staked my life."

"Crap," Keno said quietly.

"No, that's straight, kid," Hook said seriously. "This Westerman is harder'n a barrel of railroad spikes. And he runs this whole bailiwick—lock, stock, barrel, including sheriff and judge. He says cricket, they all chirp."

"I found that out near twenty years ago." Dad Tasker rapped his bony knuckles on the table. "Cross Lewis B. Westerman and you're a dead man."

Keno settled a cold, curious stare on the old man's scarred face. "Something else, too. How come you sent way to Sonora for me? You had to guess where I might be at. Just luck your Indian found me quick as he did. You could have got another man easy enough."

"Not for this job, boy. Men with both brains and cool heads don't grow on trees. This job gonna take both. You got to fool one smart ole boy—Westerman—and you slip once, you're dead. What counts most, maybe, I know you like I do Hook. Ain't neither of you would run a sandy and cross up a man."

Keno said slowly, "Hook's older than me. I'd figure..."

"Huh-uh." Hook grinned. "Wouldn't nobody believe I'm in charge. Ain't got the feel for running a job. You'll do the talking, do and say what's right for us both."

Keno shook his head wryly. "Anybody sees an honest face on either one of us, he best have his eyes looked at."

"That's where you're wrong, boy," Dad grunted. "A big insurance outfit wouldn't hire no blossoms for a man's work. You two look your parts. Tough." He leaned forward, rapping his knuckles more. "You give ear now. I want to hurt Westerman. Bad. Deep in his pride. Killing him don't make a show alongside that. This'll do it. But I need your help, boy. Half my cut's yours if you say the word."

"Quit it," Keno said irritably. He slacked back in his chair. "I'll do the job. Let's take it from the start. I want to hear the whole plan, nothing left out."

Dad and Garfield took turns talking, laying it out totally for him. Keno toyed with his cup as they talked, still not liking it. The job would be dangerous, but he had never shied from danger. He had lived it rough and hard for as long as he could remember, first with Dad and then on his own. Keno had crossed to the shady side of the law a good many times because that had been part of his raising. If there were no warrants out for him yet it was pure luck. At twenty-one he had a reputation as a bad man to cross, and one that honest people steered wide of.

What was it about this job?—a feel of something not quite right, of something left unsaid. Unable to put his finger on what, all he could do was lay the feeling to imagination.

Garfield called for a bottle. Peggott, who was out in his storeroom, yelled for Tally Jo to bring it. Garfield's eyes followed her from the kitchen to the bar to the table and back to the kitchen—he never stopped talking. For the next hour he didn't stop drinking either, as the four hashed out the fine points of the plan.

Finally Garfield got unsteadily to his feet. "Well, that should do it, all right, gen'l'men. I'll tell Westerman I've definite word of the agents being on their way. And you two will show up in three days. Now I must go down and say hello-good night to—hup!—my little Mex'can ench'lada. 'Scuse me."

He swallowed the last drop in his glass and gave Keno a bleary stare. "Seen you someplace for sure. Know I did."

"It may come back," Keno said politely.

Garfield muttered something and capped it with "Huh huh" as he headed for the kitchen door. "Go out through the back way. Shorter...."

Keno glanced at Dad. "One thing bothers me. That wolfer—Shefflin. He works for Westerman. And he's seen us here."

"Hell," Hook said, "he's seen me here many a time. After that beating, he won't be back."

"You're insurance agents," Dad said. "You work undercover most of the time. Kind of work that causes you to turn up in a lot of strange places. Anybody thinks they seen you before, stick with that story and you'll be all right."

Dad's eyes stayed on Keno as he talked. Keno wondered if it were his imagination or just a trick of the light that the usual bright malice in Dad's look seemed to intensify whenever he looked at his foster son. He had learned years ago that there was little but pure malice inside the old man: he could hate longer and harder than any Indian. His old grudge against Westerman came as no surprise; Keno didn't even feel curiosity as to its origin.

Giles Garfield had gotten delayed passing through the kitchen. Keno faintly heard his voice now: "My, you are a pretty thing."

"You stick to your little chili pepper, mister," came Tally Jo's quietly ominous answer. "And don't bother me."

"Think of that," Garfield said. "Such fire. There's a bittersweet quality in you, my dear. I always recognize that quality in a woman."

"Keep it up, mister. You're begging for it."

"Think of that," Garfield said.

There was a scuffling noise, then a dull *thwack* and a howl of pain from Garfield. "Why you goddam little bitch!"

Keno got up and walked across to the kitchen. He halted in the doorway. Garfield was bent half over, cuddling his right hand against his chest. Tally Jo stood a few wary feet away, a heavy skillet poised in her fist.

Garfield looked at Keno, his face white with shock and pain. "My God, she broke my hand!"

Keno said, "Tch tch" and shook his head. "That's funny. If I got pinched by a pee-ant like you, I'd just step on him."

He was moving forward as he spoke. Quick as a cat uncoiling, he grabbed Garfield by the collar and whirled him, then hammerlocked his left wrist behind him. Holding the luckless con man poised on his toes, his body arched painfully upward, Keno walked him to the door.

"My God!" Garfield cried. "You can't—"

Keno disagreed. Tally Jo swiftly opened the door

and he ushered Giles Garfield out on the porch, his free arm helplessly flailing.

Keno said, "See you in a few days," and lifted with all his strength, heaving Garfield upward and out. He gave a little extra twist that nosed him over in midair so that he struck the lake of mud face first.

The result satisfied even Keno's critical eye. He stepped back in and gently closed the door on Giles Garfield's ungentle commentary.

Tally Jo watched him with green eyes suddenly warmer than any feline's. "Thanks."

"Well, I owed you one. That was on my account too. Can't abide the color of his bloodshot eyes."

She didn't answer, just watched him, and Keno felt uncomfortable. He stared toward the barroom. Her voice stopped him.

"I guess all that talk you and those others was making..." She hesitated. "I suppose it's no good to say I wish you wouldn't."

"You listened, eh?"

"No!" Her eyes chilled; she half-lifted the skillet again, then lowered it. "You think I want to know all the dirty things that get talked about in this place? I don't! I don't give a damn what you do either!"

"Don't."

"I don't!" Her voice dropped suddenly. A little forlornly she added, "I just wish you wasn't doing it."

CHAPTER FIVE

Three days later Keno and Hook rode off the last flats below the timber-clad slopes on the northeast edge of the valley. A blinding red sun was dropping behind the peaks; a cool brush of evening air stroked off their heights.

Both men were muffled in drab blanket coats. Keno had exchanged his Mexican rig for an outfit of flannel shirt, well-worn corduroy breeches, and scuffed high lace-boots. This was to give him a "company man" look, Pop had said. Keno had kept his black ranchero hat. Hook, as second man, wore his usual nondescript range clothes.

They rocked in their saddles with a look of slumped weariness that wasn't feigned. Their horses showed the strain of a long day's ride.

This morning they'd ridden across the valley clear to its far south end, afterward circling widely back and around to reach their destination. They were men who had come a long way; they had to look it.

They were close by now to the massive promontory they'd have to ascend. It rose out of the foothills like a craggy loaf and was cloaked with green-dark pines for half its height. Above that, the

timber straggling off in ragged fingers, it rounded
into a bald fawn-colored summit. A few threads of
smoke tattered into the windy sky up there, the
only signs of habitation.

Hook reined up, lifting his hand. "Hear something?"

"Uh-huh. Horses. Two?"

"Yeah."

They halted, eased their pistols in their holsters,
and waited. Two riders were coming at a brittle clip
off the rocky flats to their right, and now they
skirted into sight. A man. And a woman, side-
saddle.

"Garfield," Hook grunted. "His lady love, huh?"

They put their mounts forward to meet the two.

"Why, Dave!" Garfield yelped in overdone greeting. "Dave Landry!"

He stuck out his hand—the left one. The right
hand, Keno noticed with pleasure, was heavy with
bandages, though not in a sling. Apparently, if Tally
Jo hadn't broken it, she had come close.

"Howdy, Giles," Keno drawled. "You remember
Rafe Catlett."

"Of course!" Garfield gave Hook a left-hand
shake. "Might have known the governor would send
both of you fellows. I asked for the company's two
best men."

All this pleasantry was for the benefit of the au-
burn-haired girl who rode beside Garfield.

Handsome, not pretty, was the word for Luana
Westerman's strongly molded features. At first
glance, the qualities of "sweet" and "quiet" came to
mind. Then you noticed the firmness of mouth and
chin. They belonged to a young woman who, at
nineteen, damned well knew her own mind. It was
always a mistake, Keno knew, to understand people
like that too quickly. For the rest, she was medium
height with an almost boyishly slim (but unmistak-

ably feminine) figure set off by a modish riding habit of gray cashmere that matched her eyes.

Keno wasn't sure, but he thought he detected a small puzzlement in her face as they were introduced. Her eyes searched his face as if trying to recall something. Then the expression faded; she gave him a pleasant smile and greeting, the same for Hook.

"That's the place, ain't it?" Hook jerked a nod toward the loaf-shaped promontory. "Figured that was it from the directions we got back in town, but don't see no road leading this way."

"No road," Garfield said cheerily. "Just a foot trail leading up. Luana and I always come down for a ride in the hills around this time of day; we were just heading back. Come on—this way."

The trail showed plainly enough as the four of them neared the gradual lift of south-flanking slope and rode up single file into the rising timber. The path wasn't only narrow and winding, it was little used. A fact that reminded Keno of what Pop had said about Westerman setting up practically a self-contained community inside his stockade walls.

The trees began to thin away. Now the trail clung in awkward angles to the face of the escarpment, not running straight up but sharply switchbacking toward the summit. In places it followed stony ledges that leaned over a sheer drop. Just looking down made your insides curdle.

"Trail's an old one," Garfield told them. "Note the chipmarks in the rock? Must have been hewn out by Indians in some forgotten time. At any rate it restricts a man to foot or horseback. Also, as you can see, a man alone up there could hold off an army."

Keno was surprised by the hearty English accent that Garfield now wore like a crisp new glove. The only Englishman Keno had ever met was a cardsharp in Brownsville who'd once been a crumb off

the upper crust. Garfield was pretty nearly that
Britisher's echo.

Luana didn't say much. She bore Garfield's un-
ending prattle with an air of good-natured toler-
ance. Lucky thing, Keno thought, for in or out of
character Garfield seemed incapable of putting a
cinch on his jaw. A downright wonder he didn't give
something away, but his stock of verbal nothings
was inexhaustible.

Keno couldn't get over it. He'd expected Luana to
be either a dim-brained chit or a spoiled, insuffer-
able snob of a rich man's daughter. Or both. Instead,
what little she said showed her to be a bright,
friendly, sensible girl who had probably never done
a questionable thing outside of getting herself engaged to Giles Garfield, né William R. Lutz.

The trail was easier to negotiate as they neared
the rounded, sun-scorched dome of the promontory.
Vast slabs of rock roofed the dome, chopping off a
rider's view on every side until, rounding a mono-
lithic boulder, they came suddenly in sight of the
stockade.

It was constructed of straight, slim pine trunks
harvested from the thick growth farther down.
These had been drawknived to join neatly together,
the bases being sunk in the ground and the tops
lashed together by a lacing of heavy rope. Above the
big double gates fronting the palisade was a block-
house tower with a wooden sunroof. Under it, a single guard lounged.

He swung alertly to his feet and moved to the
edge of the platform, his rifle casually raised.

"Couple strangers, Miss Luana?"

"It's all right, Roddy. These are the insurance
agents who are due—Mr. Landry and Mr. Catlett.
We met them down on the flats. Mr. Garfield knows
both of them."

The guard nodded lazily. He left the platform, de-

scending a ladder that dropped down behind the
stockade.

The crossbar securing the gates rattled as it was
lifted. Roddy dragged both gates wide and stood
back as they rode through.

Keno pulled over and leaned down, hand ex-
tended. "Name's Dave Landry."

"Roddy Baffin."

Baffin shook hands briefly. He was lean as a
bone, in his early thirties, with fiery hair that grew
in a high widow's peak. Taken with his gaunt grin,
it gave him a mildly Satanic look. Lights of stark-
wild impulse leaped behind his pale eyes. Keno
knew the signs. One of the gun-hungry ones.

"You the manager here?" Keno asked.

Baffin chuckled. "Might say I manage my end.
Mr. Westerman hired me and a few friends o' mine
to see after his interests."

I'll bet, Keno thought. He gave Baffin a parting
nod and nudged his mount after the others.

A horse corral was formed by a pole fence that
quartered off the corner of the stockade to their
right. They rode to the corral gate. Three men were
seated beside it, palavering in the way of men with
nothing better to do. They had that in common, and
two more things: all three were well armed and all
looked tougher than a roadhouse steak.

Mr. Baffin's friends, Keno guessed.

One of them, a gray wisp of a man dressed in
worn, shiny leather, courteously rose and doffed his
hat to Luana, then stepped to unfasten the wire
loop that secured the gate.

"Let me take your horse, *señorita.*"

Luana thanked the gray-haired little Mexican as
he helped her down. She introduced him as Bartolo
Rudirosa. The other two were Hans Vedder, a
round-faced youth with apple cheeks and close-
cropped pale hair, and a lank, mournful beanpole of
a fellow known as Jubilo.

Keno mentally dismissed the last two as competent toughs. Rudirosa was something else. Baffin seemed to be the leader, but Rudirosa, despite his years and his gauntly polite manner, was probably the really dangerous one of the four.

After turning their horses in, Keno and Hook shouldered their saddles and gear and followed the girl and Garfield across the dusty compound toward a row of shacks flanking the stockade's north wall.

As they crossed it, Keno saw that the palisade was three-sided, enclosing a good four acres of ground. The fourth side was formed by a granite rim of steep cliff that dropped away for hundreds of feet. Luana pointed out different buildings: shaft house, tool shed, mill house, cookshack, and mess hall.

Men on different jobs were continually moving back and forth on every side, and each of them had a respectfully friendly word of greeting for "Miss Luana"—just as each pointedly ignored Garfield, the smooth Britisher who was "marrying in."

Luana waved her hand at a man just emerging from the shaft house. "There's my father. Oh, Pa!"

Major Lewis Westerman was about sixty, stocky as a hogshead and brown as a coffee bean. He wore the plain black broadcloth suit and tall jackboots that seemed to be a uniform for any well-to-do rancher in the region. A dust-colored Stetson rode his thick shock of silvery hair. A drooping white mustache hid his mouth; it would be a tight, severe line, to judge by the stern brackets of weather-puckered skin at the corners.

His handshake was a perfunctory grab: he pumped your hand once and dropped it.

"Landry, eh? Pretty young for this responsible a position, ain't you?"

"Depends," Keno said. "I been through a few grinders."

Westerman's eyes made an ice-gray study of his

hard young face, not reserving judgment. A frosty hint of smile touched his lips then. "Yeah. I'd say you have, at that."

And Keno found a faint half-question in his stare—exactly the reaction he'd first seen in the daughter's face. Keno was getting irritated. Did something or other about him arouse suspicion?

No, that couldn't be. He remembered that Garfield at first meeting had thought he'd known him from somewhere. Yet he'd never seen either Garfield or the Westermans before. What the hell?

Luana said, "Pa, I was about to show Mr. Landry and Mr. Catlett to where they'll stay...."

"Good. That shack on the end has been furnished for you, gentlemen. Rest and clean up, if you like. Then I'll expect you to join us for supper. Want to hear your plans for my bullion."

Luana led them down the row of puncheon-and-tarpaper shanties that housed the mining crew. The last one in line looked no worse nor better than the rest. Luana started to pull open the slab door, which stuck. Keno gave her a hand.

The single room was equipped with two wooden cots and lumpy straw ticks, along with a wash-stand, water pitcher, and basin. Some effort had been made to arrange things for their comfort. The cots were made up with fresh sheets and clean blankets; the floor was freshly scrubbed, and the smell of lyesoap lingered.

Luana, coloring a little, said, "I want to apologize for this. I mean, Pa could have had a room fixed up for you in our house, easily as not. I've, er, tried to make things a bit more comfortable...."

"Yes'm." Hook clucked his tongue, vastly approving. "Man couldn't miss that lady touch."

She blushed more deeply and murmured something and went out, followed by Garfield. He sent them a conspiratorial wink before closing the door.

Hook sent Keno a sober glance. "That Roddy Baffin. Know him from a long time back."

Keno dropped his saddle and blanket roll at the foot of a cot and laid his rifle down too. Afterward he stripped off his coat, walked to the shaving mirror beside the washstand, and scrubbed a palm reflectively over his whiskered jaw.

"How long back? From where?"

"Arizona, twelve-thirteen years ago." Hook grunted as he peeled off his shirt over his head, expertly tugging with his hook and hand. "Roddy was the youngest waddy on the old X-Bar crew. I was top hand for that outfit and 'most any other damn cow crew you could name in the Mogollon country."

"How likely is he to remember you?"

"Hell, I dunno."

Hook had stripped to the waist. Now he came to the washstand, filled the basin, and scooped water vigorously one-handed over his head. The great muscles of his arms and shoulders rolled under the pale skin.

"Listen," Keno said flatly. "I'll take a fifty-fifty chance any time. Even a sixty-forty chance, stakes are big enough. But odds that run ninety-ten always bother me."

Hook straightened up, spluttering. The wet hair plastered to his bullet head gleamed like a seal's pelt. "Yeah, that's right, ain't it?" He reached for the towel. "I was Jim Blanding back then. Here I'm Rafe Catlett. Not so good, that boy gets remembering."

"Not good at all," Keno said. "Look, if the odds are wrong, better we drop everything now and pull out while we're in one piece. Figure up the odds, Hook."

Hook patted himself dry, scowling judiciously. "Well," he said at last, "I figure they're fair enough. Roddy, hell, he was just a green kid them days—seventeen or so. Anyhow I left the X-Bar a couple

weeks after he signed on. We both worked around
the same general area for a year or so after that,
but never for the same outfit again—never seen
each other only in town once or twice. Me, hell, I
was younger too. Had both arms then. You be surprised how different a man looks with a hook. Not
to say a few years on him."

Keno weighed the answer, finally nodding. "All
right. We stick. But we play everything damn close.
And we keep all our eyes open."

"Hell, yes. Now let's finish up and get over to that
Major's. Said supper, didn't he? My belly is playing
tag wrassle with my backbone."

CHAPTER SIX

Though they were living in this rough camp at present, the Westermans were by no means roughing it. They had a sprawling, well-built multiroomed cabin to themselves.

Admitted by a middle-aged colored woman who said she was Hessie, Keno and Hook found themselves in an oasis of modest grandeur. The log walls of the dining room-parlor were decorated with bright Navajo blankets, old flintlock weapons, trophy heads of bear, deer, and bighorn sheep. A settee and armchairs were covered in fine dark leather. A long table was set with bone china and silverware that gleamed against the snowy luxury of a damask tablecloth.

Hook was overawed. "What," he muttered, "do you reckon their *regular* diggings look like?"

Luana came out from a back room wearing a dress of crackling blue satin. It belled full in the skirt, but hugged her slim upper body. Tightly outlined, her breasts were small and high, her waist narrow as a young willow. Her smile made her almost beautiful.

"Sit down, please. A drink, gentlemen? Bourbon or brandy...?"

They both said bourbon. Keno sank uneasily onto the deep leather of the settee. Hook, even more skittery, sat ramrod-straight on the edge of the cushions, his hat damply crushed between his fists.

"Nice little shack," Keno said.

"Isn't it?"

She laughed, standing at the oak sideboard and filling two man-size tumblers from a decanter of bourbon that Keno guessed was too rich for a poor man's blood.

"Pa likes to be next to all his operations. Cattle, mines, whatever. And this is about the biggest windfall ever for the Westermans. So I'd reckon we'll be here till snow flies. Meantime, why not enjoy all the comforts of home? Home's down in the valley... our biggest ranch."

"Would think you'd get bored way up here."

"Not at all. Not with Giles here." She handed each man his drink. "There's lots to do, such as riding and fishing. I'm a girl who likes plenty of men around. Cool up here, too. Midsummer down in the valley is—what's the old saying?—great for men and dogs, death on women and horses."

Major Westerman and Giles Garfield entered from one of the back rooms, both impeccably dressed for dinner.

Hessie served the meal, which was delicious. The Major carved the roast saddle of elk and forked generous portions onto each plate. There were mashed potatoes, peas, pan gravy, thick wedges of apple pie, even fresh cream with the coffee. After weeks of sorry grub, Keno didn't ask questions: he simply followed Hook's example and ate his way through seconds and thirds.

The Major passed around a box of Havanas, motioned Hessie to refill the coffee cups, and clipped off his cigar tip with a cutter on a gold chain, lighted up, and sighed out a fragrant cloud.

"Down to business, gentlemen, eh? Like to see your papers if I might."

Luana smiled. "He thinks he can't be too careful, even if you are friends of Giles's."

Westerman harrumphed and leafed slowly through the sheaf of beautifully forged identification papers that Keno produced from an inside coat pocket. Keno's palms sweated as he watched the mine owner's face. He relaxed only slightly when, a few minutes later, Westerman gave a curtly satisfied nod and handed back the papers.

"Very good. Now, boy, I'd like to hear all your plans for getting that bullion out of here safely."

"Sorry, sir," Keno said in a softly blunt tone. "We ain't at liberty to tell you."

The Major frowned. "What's that?"

"Sir, our company underwrites this cargo. Our duty, Rafe's and mine, is to see it gets where it's going. Look at it from where we stand. You know our plans, you could have your own men—say, them toughs we seen out by the gate—lay for us and rob us. Company'd have to pay you the amount that was stolen, and you'd have the gold too. Policy, sir. Nothing personal."

The Major's lips stirred for the second time with the faint frosty smile. "Good. Damned good. But my real concern is, what if somebody else tries for the gold? I gather there's just you two escorting it out of here. Course I don't know what-all precautions you'll be taking."

"All that's confidential, sir. Once we're away from this valley, we'll be joined by an armed escort...I won't say where. But we didn't want to send a big gun-hung crew here to your mine. Be like waving a red flag to every hardcase in the territory."

The Major nodded. "Exactly why I took on your company. Giles has assured me this is old stuff to you."

"Yes, sir. I'll tell you this. We got detail maps of

the country from the U. S. Land Office. Every mile
of the route planned. Could damn near—beg par-
don, miss—name you the place and hour we'll have
this bullion on a train East."

"Good. Good." The Major didn't smile again, but a
chain of rapid puffs on his cigar showed he was im-
pressed.

They had passed the big hurdle all right, Keno
thought. All the same he had to keep up an iron
guard for the rest of the evening.

Westerman was no fool. In the most casual talk
he'd interject an occasional shrewdly oblique comment which called on Keno to dredge up a right answer, and fast. It taxed his ingenuity and nerve to
the limit. If he faltered just once, let one crack show
in his toughly seasoned front, he could touch a
nerve end of suspicion. At best seed a doubt in Westerman's mind.

Meantime he was called on to swallow each of
many double bourbons that Westerman poured for
his guests ("No reason for you boys not to drink tonight, is there?") while he fixed every atom of con-
centration on controlling his tongue.

Maybe, behind his apparent acceptance of them,
Westerman really was suspicious. The possibility
began to worry Keno. Maybe he could throw the
mine owner off. If he and Hook were working something shady, they'd be anxious to get away from
here quickly, wouldn't they?

When a lull came in the conversation, Keno said
idly, "We ought to be turning in pretty quick, Rafe
and me. Man gets used to rising with the birds, this
business. By the way, Major, wonder if you'd mind
we stay over here one day? We come a long ways
and we figured on a day just resting up. It fits into
our plan. Man's got to be fresh on a job like this."

Westerman thought it was a fine idea.

Keno didn't like it a little bit. Every additional
hour they stayed increased the risk they ran. Yet

his suggestion did seem to relax any small suspicion
of the Major's. At least it ended the sly questioning.

As he saw them to the door, Westerman said,
"Like both you fellows to be over here after breakfast. We'll weigh out the gold and transfer it to the
packs—get everything ready for your departure,
eh?"

As the two tramped back to their quarters, Hook
was weaving a little, softly cursing.

"Jesus. Another o' them doubles and the top o'
my head would of blowed clean off. I was scared he'd
start pitching questions to me."

"Reckon he didn't figure all that fine booze'd faze
a tough old hand like you," Keno said gravely. "You
looked solemn as a circuit preacher."

"Good reason," Hook growled. "I was purely
numb, is why."

Next morning they joined the mining crew in the
mess hall. The men crowded the long puncheon
tables and benches. Keno and Hook found themselves seated on the bench across from Roddy Baffin
and his gunnies.

"Morning," Keno said.

Bartolo Rudirosa said, *"Buenos días,"* in a whis-
per-dry voice.

"Morning, Landry." Baffin gave a lean-faced grin.
"And Mister—Catlett, ain't it? Catlett?"

"Yeah," Hook said around a mouthful of griddle-
cake.

That was all, but Keno wondered. Afterward, as
he and Hook crossed the compound toward the Westerman cabin, Hook muttered:

"That goddam Baffin. You reckon he was trying
to spook me?"

"Maybe he wants you to spook yourself."

Hook scratched his jaw. "Maybe it didn't mean
nothing. How did he look to you?"

"Quit it," Keno said mildly. "We come this far. Let's keep our heads and ride it out."

Keno's knock at the door was answered by Hessie, who said that the Major was in his office out back. At her direction, they tramped around to a small log shanty connected by a turkey trot to the main cabin.

The door was open. The Major was squatted on his heels in front of a giant old-fashioned iron safe that was dented and battered from long service. He was pulling out a number of small heavy canvas sacks that made a solid clink as he dropped them one by one on a big scale set on the floor beside him.

He glanced up. "Come in, boys. Was just weighing the stuff out. Have to apportion it so we won't overload the mules."

They spent the next half hour helping Westerman carefully weigh out the bullion. It totaled up to roughly seven hundred and eighty pounds, or in the neighborhood of two hundred thousand dollars. A fair cut short of the more than a quarter million that Garfield had estimated, but a hefty sum all the same.

They packed the small bags into larger canvas sacks that could be slung from a mule's back. Keno hefted each fist-sized poke gingerly, feeling an involuntary tingling of his fingertips. Seeing this much gold at once would put butterflies in a man's gut even if he had no intention of stealing it.

They found that the entire load distributed evenly into six of the large sacks.

"Three mules will do the job," the Major said with satisfaction. "When do you plan on packing it out, Landry?"

"Figure to start out first light tomorrow," Keno said. "Time it's sun-up, we'll be off this roost and across the flats and over in them foothills way east of your valley."

Westerman nodded his approval. "Figured that

much. Quickest way out of the valley. You'll save miles, and there ain't a soul living between here and there outside a few Mex sheepmen. But once you're in them foothills, there'll be damned tough going."

Keno grinned. "That's right, Major. But we got the route laid out from there so an Injun couldn't track us. We ain't in no hurry, and that's damned well all you're going to know."

Westerman chuckled thinly.

A moccasined foot grated softly; a man's gaunt shadow fell across the bare rectangle of sunlight angling through the doorway. Westerman came stiffly to his feet, a cold anger in his face.

"Shefflin. Who the devil told you to come here?"

"Oh, nobody. Nobody at all, Major." Bone Shefflin stepped softly into the room, scratching his whiskered jaw with his good hand. "The boys at the gate, they know me good. Told 'em I had 'nother pack o' wolfskins I brung in for the bounty, so they let me right in."

"And told you to come straight here, I suppose?" the Major snapped.

Keno had glided to his feet in one fluid movement as Shefflin had come through the door. A backward step put him slightly behind the Major and to his right. His hand was free, an inch or so from the gunbutt.

But he didn't touch it. Not yet. Let Shefflin say the word.

He shot a single glance at Hook that warned him, *Hold still.* It wasn't needed. Hook remained sitting on his haunches with a frozen look on his face, not stirring a muscle.

Keno did not blame him. It was simply a paralyzing stroke of luck. His own mouth was too dry even to curse.

He thought fast. Let Shefflin say his piece. Then grab Westerman before he could turn. Hammerlock his arm. Westerman, a gun muzzle at his neck, would be their passport out of this place.

Shefflin's gaze had already lighted on him. Now it slid to Hook and back again. He continued to gently scratch his jaw, a vague grin on his lips. His other arm was in the bulky sling. He seemed to hesitate.

"No, sir," he answered Westerman. "That nigger keeps house for you, I ast her where you was. Said she didn't know and slammed the door in my face. Downright uppity mean, that nigger. Figured you might be in this here office, so I come around here."

"All right," Westerman said with a wintry disdain. "You're here." He motioned at the bulging sacks. "You know what these are?"

"That don't take no tall guessing, Major." He grinned at Keno and Hook. "Sure a caution who these fellers might be, though. Ain't seen 'em about. Friends o' yourn?"

So that's how it'll be, Keno thought. The cold knot in his gut did not ease. Whatever was in Shefflin's head, he had the pure animal cunning of the wolves he trapped. And was far more dangerous.

Westerman curtly introduced both "insurance agents." Shefflin held out a dirty hand. "Purely pleased to meetchez," he said toothily. "Mr. Landry —Mr. Catlett. C'n I bring in them wolfskins now, Major?"

"You'll get your bounty pay later," Westerman said curtly. "Listen to me, Shefflin. I'm going to keep you in this stockade till day after tomorrow. You understand? You'll be assigned a shack apart so you won't gripe the men with your wolfer stink. You—"

"Howcum, Major?"

"You stinking thick-headed fool. Because you've seen too much. You ain't getting out of my sight till twenty-four hours after I know these men and this gold are out safely."

"Sure," Shefflin said amiably, still scratching. "Feller can't be too keerful. Even 'round his friends he can't."

Westerman grimaced. "Ahh... get out of here. If you want breakfast, see Coosie. Maybe he'll set out more scraps."

"Heh heh. Allus said you was a powerful kind sort, Major. Mind if I kinder mosey 'round the diggings?"

"Shefflin, I don't give a good damn what you do. Just stay out of the way. And if you value your dirty hide, don't try to leave the stockade."

The wolfer shuffled to the door with a woodsman's gaunt peculiar grace. Pausing, he gave Keno a sly stare.

"'Spect I will see you fellers again. Today."

With the softest of chuckles, he went out.

CHAPTER SEVEN

"Trouble was," Hook commented dourly, "you busted the wrong part on that wolfer's stringy carcass when you had the chance."

"Hell of a mistake," Keno agreed.

"Maybe we oughta go find the son of a bitch. Straighten this out now."

"Huh-uh." Keno sat on the ground with his knees drawn up, twirling a twig between his fingers. "Let him make the move. He will."

It was midafternoon. They had spent the morning idling about the camp, killing time by inspecting the machinery and even making a tour of the main shaft. After the noon meal they had taken a siesta, stretching out on the ground in the dusty parallelogram of shade thrown by the mess hall on its north side. Now, an hour later, they were sitting in the same place, quietly talking over their situation.

Moodily, Keno stared across the palisade toward the black-green wall of mountain range sawtoothing against a sky of hot, pale indigo. All they could do was hold on tight and go ahead as planned. Shefflin hadn't tipped their hand yet, and he'd had plenty of time.

Hook was sprawled on his back with one leg cocked across the other knee, hand and hook folded on his chest and hat shading his eyes. Suddenly he raised himself and thumbed back his hat, murmuring, "Look at that."

Keno turned his head.

Roddy Baffin, tailed by his three friends, was coming across the compound. They were headed straight for Keno and Hook; there was something purposeful in their approach.

Keno snapped the twig in his fingers and eased to his feet. Hook stood too.

Baffin hauled up a dozen feet away, grinning whitely. "Mostly I don't go prodding a man about his business. Only your partner, now. I been thinking about him."

"Have you."

"Yeah. I know this ole one-wing from somewheres. Just can't peg where. Keeps bothering me, see. Maybe if he answers a few questions for me, I won't be bothered no more."

Keno sized the way Baffin was facing them. Bartolo Rudirosa stood off to his right; Vedder and Jubilo were spread out on his left. Nothing casual in this confrontation. Baffin meant business.

Hook grinned, tucking his thumb into his broad brass-studded belt. "Boy, I'd say you have got my face crossed with someone else."

"Don't reckon," Baffin said. "Tell you another thing. I got a deep feeling about your memory being a sight sharper'n mine. Be obliged you refresh me. Where was it?"

Hook shook his head, still grinning.

Bartolo Rudirosa ran a finger along the shiny-worn leather of his gunbelt. "Don't be funny, my friend. We are not being funny."

"Show him how funny we ain't being," Baffin said. "Hans, Jubilo. Show him."

Rudirosa palmed his pistol in a split instant, leveling it on Keno's chest.

"You don't move, Landry. You don't bat the winker."

Keno smiled faintly. He raised his shoulders and let them fall. He hadn't been wrong about Rudirosa.

Vedder moved forward, waddling a little on his chunky legs, and lifted Keno's gun from the holster. He tossed it to the gravelly soil some yards away. He did the same for Hook.

Jubilo put his watery stare on Keno. "You stand aside."

Keno took a few lazy steps to the right, his hands cocked on his hips. He figured, knowing Hook, that they had a surprise in store.

The six of them were cut off here from the rest of the compound. They stood on a five-yard oblong of bare ground between the mess hall and the north wall of the palisade. Nobody was likely to notice a scuffle.

Hook stood flatfooted, faintly grinning yet, his great-ape shoulders and arms very loose. Vedder and Jubilo came in on him from two sides: Vedder almost as powerfully thickset as Hook, Jubilo towering gauntly above them both, but tough with stringy muscle.

"Watch that goddam hook," Vedder muttered an instant before Jubilo closed with a rush on Hook's right.

Hook simply swung his steel member up in a savage backhand swing. The heavy hook rapped solidly against Jubilo's forehead. He spun away with a howl, clapping his hands over his face.

Vedder lunged at Hook from his other side. Not moving otherwise, Hook just turned his shoulder and leaned his weight. Vedder's chest collided with the solid bulwark of Hook's shoulder. He grunted with the slamming impact, then backpedaled two steps in a kind of rebound.

Hook, making it all look casual, straight-armed Vedder on the point of his jaw with the clublike heel of his palm. Vedder sat down hard on the ground.

Jubilo was bent over, clutching his head with both hands. The hook's rounded arc, not its needle point, had met his forehead. But that had been enough to open an inch-wide split in the skin. He bellowed like a wounded buffalo as he tried to paw away the blood showering into his eyes.

Hook gave him an unconcerned glance, then swung over toward Vedder. The thickset youth still sat on his fat rear, trying awkwardly to pull his gun.

Hook planted his boot on the center of Vedder's chest and drove him backward against the ground, pinning him. Hook bent a little. He waved the bright hook gently back and forth under Vedder's nose.

"That wasn't worth a good sweat, sonny. You see this? I could just as easy have give that long drink of water the hook end in his eye. And you. I could o' gutted you down clean as a split channel cat before you got near enough to bump me."

"One-wing. Figure you can beat this too?"

Baffin had pulled his gun now, bringing it up to fix on Hook's head.

"He don't need to," Keno said reasonably. "You ain't going to use it."

Baffin eyed him with a cold, baffled anger. Then rammed the gun back in his holster and laughed. "Pretty salty pair, ain't you?"

"Not right yet," Keno said arrogantly. "We're just apt to turn that way."

Baffin laughed again. He looked at Hook. "I'll remember, bucko. When and where. You depend on it."

He swung away. Rudirosa let his gun off cock and holstered it. "Maybe, *señor,* another time. Eh?"

"You pick it," Keno said.

Vedder climbed warily to his feet and started after them. So did Jubilo, holding a bandanna to his brow. Keno and Hook watched the four cross out of sight behind the cookshack. Hook picked up the guns and handed Keno his.

"Suppose'n he tells Westerman?"

"Tells Westerman what? He's got a bug up his rear about your face seems familiar? What of it?"

"More'n that," Hook growled. "He knows something don't smell right. Sure enough that he sicced them two on to beat the truth outen me."

"Sure. But why? Because he needs more'n a bad smell in his nose to show Westerman. Garfield vouched for us. We got enough good-looking paper to pass with the old man. All that's solid. Baffin ain't got a solid fact in his poke."

"I ain't sure of but one thing. I need a drink."

Keno slapped him on the shoulder. "Brought a good bottle from Mexico. Still in my saddlebag. Let's have a look at it."

They walked across the compound to their shanty. Keno noticed as he reached for the door that it was off latch. Yet he remembered hooking the latch this morning. Palming his gun up swiftly, he pushed open the door and stepped in.

Bone Shefflin was sprawled at ease on a cot, his dirty boots crossed on the rumpled blanket. He had found Keno's bottle of tequila and was in the middle of a long pull, gurgling it down like water instead of liquid fire.

Keno went over and gently lifted the bottle from his hand. "How you know we was here?"

"Ast." Shefflin chuckled blearily. "Where's them insurance fellers at, I ast."

Hook took the bottle from Keno and stared in outrage at the three inches of colorless liquid remaining. "You hairy son of a bitch," he said ominously. "Get the hell offen my bed or you'll be eating the rest, bottle too."

Shefflin lounged to his feet with an insolent confidence. "I know what you fellers is cutting. I want a piece of it."

"Want to make it plainer?" Keno said.

Shefflin nodded at Hook. "His name ain't Catlett. I seen him hanging around Peggott's a good two-three weeks before you come. Him and that ole man. They cooked it up, didn't they? Then sent along for you."

"You better make sense," Keno said. "We work for a big insurance outfit. We always scout out a territory before we take a job. Do it under different names."

"That don't wash, boy. That limey feller who is Miss Luana's beau, he met this one-arm and the ole man at Peg's more'n once. I seen 'em together. They was all working out something for sure, but I don't reckon it was no insurance deal. Course if you say 'twas, we c'n go talk to the Major and see how he feels on't."

Keno glanced at Hook, who shrugged. "Said you busted the wrong thing on him."

"I guess he's in," Keno said. "How hungry you feel, Shefflin?"

"That Garfield," Shefflin scratched his ribs meditatively. "He's in too, huh? And that ole man. Hell, I ain't greedy. A fifth'll do each man, hey?"

"Wonder if we couldn't bust the right thing here and now?" Hook said hopefully. "Say it was an accident."

"Seems we're over a barrel," Keno said. "You'll meet us for your split then. Same place the others do."

Shefflin shook his head. "Not hardly, boy. How I know you'll tell ole Bone the right place? When you two go outa here, I go with you."

"That might take some doing, seeing Westerman won't let you go till twenty-four hours after us."

"I figgered that." Shefflin stabbed a dirty thumb

at him. "You got maps and suchlike, but it ain't the same as knowing a piece of country. You're afeared you might get lost outen them hills. You need a man who knows the terr'tory first hand. Been talking to me, tell the Major. You want ole Bone 'long for a guide."

"Seeing how he trusts you," Keno said dryly, "how you reckon he'll buy that?"

"Don't matter how. He'll buy." Shefflin grinned wolfishly. "You gonna see to it, boy. 'Cause without he does, you two gonna both be dead."

That evening, Hook swallowed the last of the tequila for "nerve medicine." It must have been effective, for he was sawing wood within a few minutes.

That, as much as anything, helped keep Keno from dropping off. He restfully twisted in his blankets for awhile. Finally he threw them off, yanked on his boots, and let himself quietly out of the shanty.

He headed away from the squalid layout of shacks, out toward the cliff side of the compound. He rolled a smoke as he strolled, enjoying the high, cool night and finally halting by the rounded bulge of granite that lipped over a vast drop.

Maybe he was worried about nothing. Apparently Baffin's suspicions had run up a blind alley. The promise of his cut would insure Shefflin's silence...and Westerman had given a reluctant consent to Bone's accompanying them. Another few hours and they'd be on their way out, carrying a fortune in raw gold.

Somebody kicked a pebble. Keno turned unhurriedly, glancing toward the deep shadows to his left and back. Somebody. He flicked his cigarette away and squared around, ready for anything.

"Trouble sleeping, too, Mr. Landry?" Luana asked. "I don't blame you."

She walked into the open moonlight, a shawl

hugged around her shoulders. "Brr. Cold, isn't it? I saw you from the window of my room and thought I'd join you." She smiled. "I have to confess to a deep curiosity."

Keno eyed her guardedly. "Yes'm."

"Where are you from, Dave?"

"Anywhere. Everywhere."

Luana laughed. "As a born Westerner, I know it's bad form—if not downright unsafe—to ask. But I do have a reason. I've had the oddest feeling since we met...could it be possible I met you in the East? Perhaps at a party?"

"Don't reckon we ever shared in the same party, miss. Though you can't tell. My work takes a man most everywhere."

"I suppose it does." She gazed thoughtfully across the weirdly lit landscape below them. "Tell me... how well do you know Giles?"

Keno shrugged. "Not much."

"I thought you were friends."

"I work for his old man and other people. We know each other good enough. Wouldn't call us friends."

"Oh. I thought..." She broke off with a small embarrassed laugh. "I thought you might be able to shed a little light...but never mind."

Keno knew well enough what she meant. Again he wondered how this bright, quick girl had been taken in by such a lightweight fake as Garfield. And then he thought, *I wonder if she was?*

It prompted him to ask, "How much do *you* know about him? Garfield?"

She gave him a swift, searching look. "That's rather forward." Then sighed, shaking her head. "But I did ask for it, didn't I? And you do know Giles, so why pretend? You know how he is. So like a little boy in some ways. I—I wonder sometimes whether he'll ever grow up."

Keno didn't comment.

After a moment she added quietly, "And I know that he's not faithful, if that's what you're thinking. I'm sure you are."

"Does it matter?"

"No. Not in the least. I love him, you see. But you can't blame me for being curious. It's just that I know so little about Giles, really. And that's strange—as much talking as he ordinarily does."

Somebody was coming from the direction of the house, whistling as he came. "Oh Lordy," Luana whispered. "I hope that's not Pa! He'll skin me alive for being out now."

It was Garfield.

"Evening, Dave," he said genially. He slid an arm around Luana's shoulders and hugged her, giving Keno a wink above her head. "Charming girl, isn't she?"

The way he said it made Keno feel like hitting him.

"Are you spying on me, Giles?" she asked lightly.

"Certainly," Garfield beamed. "Heard you leave your room and go out. You shouldn't be out in this camp of roughs, my dear—at night and alone."

"But I'm not. Mr. Landry was out here and I wanted to speak to him, Giles."

"Oh? What about?"

"You, of course."

"Huh huh," Garfield said. "I think we'd better get back to the house before we catch our death. Night, Landry."

Keno watched them go. He liked the girl and felt sorry for her. But he couldn't do a damned thing for her. Except one. And she wouldn't thank him for that.

CHAPTER EIGHT

After he returned to the shanty and rolled into his bunk, sleep came quickly. Dead and dreamless sleep. It lasted for perhaps an hour.

Keno had the faculty of waking as an animal would. At once, and with all his senses alert. The habit was ingrained by his way of life; it was survival habit.

And at roughly midnight a sound woke him. He wasn't sure on the instant what it had been, but his brain and senses did a rapid-fire cataloguing of just about every auditory factor in his vicinity.

It was full dark. His internalized sleep clock said that he'd slept for an hour. Hook was still snoring in the other cot. But these were almost unconscious notations. What seized his attention were the narrow pencils of light seeping through the cracks between the vertical door puncheons.

Swiftly and silently he sat up and rolled sideways, reaching for his forty-five, which he'd laid on the washstand inside easy reach. But his groping did not locate the gun at once, and then it was too late.

The door was kicked open. A lantern flared in a

man's raised fist, funneling a sickly light through the room.

"Hold it like that, boy," drawled Roddy Baffin's voice.

Keno froze with his hand on the stand's rough top an inch from his gun. He blinked the first blinding wash of light from his eyes as Hook reared up on his elbows mumbling, "What t'hell?"

Baffin came through the door first, the lantern lifted high. Rudirosa followed. Both had their guns out, covering the shack's occupants. Next Giles Garfield, his face resembling a blob of half-melted suet, came stumbling in. He was propelled none too gently by Major Lewis Westerman's hand between his shoulders.

Westerman halted at the foot of Keno's cot. His iron-colored eyes held yellow pinpoints of light. An unfired cigar was clamped in a corner of his mouth. As he removed it to speak, Keno took a kind of outraged initiative by cutting in on him:

"What the hell is this, Major?"

"I ain't sure of nothing yet, boy. You just hold your jaw." He motioned brusquely toward Baffin. "He come to me with a story. Says he's been studying all day on where he seen your partner before. It just come to him, and he figured it was important enough to roust me out."

Hook gave Baffin a sleepy blinking stare, then looked with a consummate groggy innocence at the Major. "Story? What t'hell story?"

"Tell him," Westerman said curtly.

"Why, I finally recalled," Baffin murmured with his cold smile. "The old X-Bar. I wasn't hardly over knee britches then. Only your name wa'n't Catlett them days. It was Jim Blanding. You was a sight slimmer and had little more hair, was all. And both arms."

Hook yawned slightly and gave Baffin an owlish,

half-comprehending scowl. "Sure, I was Blanding. Still am. What about it? His name ain't Landry either. We don't use no real names on these jobs. Use different ones each job matter fact."

"What about that, Baffin?"

"It's bullshit, Major, pure and plain." Baffin's grin tensed. "He knowed me, all right, when he first clapped eyes on me. It showed in his face just that once. Hell, that's what got me started thinking."

"I knowed him, all right," Hook said with a weary, contemptuous patience. "He was a runny-butt brat I wouldn't of trusted any Sunday of the year. If he didn't know me now, that was fine with me."

"There's more," Westerman said. "Rudirosa claims he's heard of a shady rider by the name of Hook Blanding. Not a name known in the states, but down in the *cantina* country they talk of him. An outlaw named Blanding who wears a hook like yours. Quite a coincidence, ain't that?"

"Nope," Hook said with a bland agility that Keno wouldn't have believed in him. "I'm him. One of my jobs for the company. This outlaw bunch had stole a big gold shipment up by Denver. It was insured and we was out money. We knew the gang was in Mexico. Only way we could recover even some o' the loot was get a man in solid with 'em. That was me."

"But you used your own name then?"

"Sure," Hook lied cheerfully. "Had to. One of that bunch knowed me from years ago in Arizona."

Westerman turned slowly on his heel and rammed his hands in his hip pockets. He walked to the door, head bent, chewing his dead cigar, then came back. His icy eyes probed Keno's face.

"So your company made out that fancy set of papers under some assumed names? Eh?"

"That's how it was, Major. Believe it or don't." Keno shrugged, showing only a faint irritation.

"You got a choice, and it's all on a man's word. Baffin's or ours."

Westerman shook his head slowly. "No choice. No choice at all. You think I'll gamble a fortune on any man's word?"

"You was willing to, seems." Keno nodded at Garfield. "On his word. If we're liars, so's he."

"Exactly." Westerman clipped out his words like a pistol hammer snapping. "He's here for that reason. Well, Giles. What do you have to say? Stop shaking, boy, and speak up."

Garfield was in his shirtsleeves; his clothes were disheveled, his hair mussed, as though he'd been yanked forcibly from his bed without explanation. From what Pop had said, Westerman would be just that rough if he had an idea he'd been played for a fool.

"Sir..." Garfield's teeth were chattering with cold or plain fear. He tried for an echo of outraged dignity, but the words came fluttering out with a phlegmy squeak. "This is fantastic! You know who my family is! The people I consorted with in the East! Why, you've known me for two years. Surely you're not taking the word of a common ruffian—over—"

"There was no doubt before," Westerman cut in curtly. "No reason to doubt. Different now. I never beat around the bush, boy. Not when there's questions raised that want straight, plain-out answers. I mean to damn well get 'em before an ounce of that bullion leaves this stockade. Get that, Mr. Landry —or whatever your name is?"

"Up to you, Major." Keno shrugged again. "Speaking just for me, I could use a few days of doing nothing. Only thing, the company has spent a lot of time and money setting up this fancy-ass scheme for getting your gold out East. Everything's been timed down pretty fine. They ain't going to cheer you for throwing a wrench in the works."

"If there's a plan. Or a company, for that matter. And if there is, whether you two are its accredited agents." Westerman kept staring grimly, trying to crack Keno's bored young mask. "I'll ride down to Pecas tomorrow and fire off some telegrams. The answers I get may bear you out. If they don't..."

Keno nodded sleepily. "Anything you say. I can use the rest. Just make it clear to the company this wasn't my idea, will you?"

"Meantime," Westerman snapped, "you two'll stay here, right in this shanty. A padlock'll be put on the door. There'll be a guard outside. With orders to shoot if you try to break out." His eyes were brittle as slate. "I want you to damned well understand that."

Baffin, his lips curled faintly up at the corners, said in an amused tone, "There's this here future son-in-law. What about him?"

"He'll stay here with 'em. You or one of your men will stand guard here. Another on the gate, as usual."

Garfield's face was slightly greenish. "You can't be serious, sir," he managed to croak.

"Boy—" Westerman swung around to squarely face him. There was a hard, open dislike in his face, and Keno guessed this was his first betrayal of real feeling toward the man his daughter had settled on. "Boy, you vouched for these two. And that's the least of what you done."

"But sir—!"

Westerman chopped a thick hand in the air. "Nothing's settled yet. I heard all the stories. Too damn many of 'em. I'll have the truth quick enough. Meantime it won't hurt you to spend a night in here. If you give me the right of things, you got no worries. But if you been running a sandy on my girl, boy. If you been lying..."

He let it hang that way. With a flat, unemotional emphasis. Then jerked a nod at Baffin:

"Search 'em. Their stuff too. Clean out everything that could make a weapon."

Baffin's search was swift and expert. He didn't miss a thing. He gathered up their Winchesters and Colts, their sheath knives, pocket knives, and razors, and a small hide-out pistol Keno wore strapped to a boot. He appropriated a shaving mirror and the tequila bottle: broken glass could be deadly. The cabin had no windows.

He and Westerman went out, carrying the weaponry. Rudirosa was left with the prisoners.

The Mexican set his narrow shoulders against the wall and crossed his arms, fist tilted to hold his gun carelessly leveled on them. His eyes were strange: pale blue, faded and disillusioned and unblinking.

"We are alone, *señores*. Maybe you say to me what is the truth? I'm curious."

"Go to hell, Bartolo," Keno said calmly.

"Ah." Rudirosa's whispery chuckle. "What a pity, young rooster. We are more *hombre,* you and me, than any of these. It would be good to find out who is most *hombre.*"

In Spanish, Keno said insolently, "You think that is a contest, Grandfather?"

Rudirosa's eyes flared, glinting. "The old cock's spurs are sharp, my rooster. Do not mistake."

In a few minutes the sleepy, complaining camp carpenter showed up to attach a heavy hasp and staple to the outside door and frame. Afterward a padlock was added and the three prisoners left alone.

Keno heard Baffin's voice outside:

"Hans, you take first watch here. I'll take the gate. Jube and the Mex'll spell us around three."

Footsteps going away.

Keno prowled around each wall, testing it with his weight. The shack was solidly built of green logs. They had no tool for cutting, prying, or digging. Maybe their combined weights could force the split-log door, but Vedder was waiting.

A hell of a pretty kettle.

Garfield was nearly in tears. "His own daughter's fiancé! And he locks me up like—"

"Another common crook," Hook gibed. "You reckon he'd leave a tricky partner like you on the outside to dream up more tricks?"

"He never did like me," Garfield mumbled.

"I wonder why."

"Muzzle it, you two," Keno murmured. "Or Westerman won't need to go to no telegraph line for his proof. As it is, we got time. Anyway a day or so."

Time. What good was it? They used it to mutter *sotto voce* notions and schemes whose futility was transparent.

An hour dragged by.

Keno lay on his cot in a half-doze. It was an old knack he had, using any lulls to marshal his faculties. It kept his reflexes fresh, his wits sharp.

Hook and Garfield were restless and unsleeping. Yet it was Keno who caught the soft telltale sound of steps approaching the shack. He identified Bone Shefflin's lurching moccasined tread before the wolfer spoke.

"Hoddy, cousin."

Keno raised himself and moved silently to the door, laying his ear against it. He motioned the others to keep still.

"Get the hell out of here," said Vedder.

"That's purely no way to talk," Shefflin said in an injured tone. "I was just taking the night air and seen you—"

There was an explosive grunt from Vedder.

"You just stand steady, cousin," Shefflin said softly. "This ain't no water pipe in your fat belly. You sing out and I bust you wide open."

"What the hell is this?" Vedder asked shakily.

"You got the key to this here padlock?"

"Baffin's got it."

"Turn around."

A flat, wicked crack of metal on flesh and bone. Vedder's head rapped against the door as he fell forward; next faint sounds indicated that Shefflin was easing the man's flaccid weight to the ground.

"Shefflin?"

"Plumb here, Mr. Landry. I'm a-gonna ram this ranny's gun barrel through the padlock and bust her clean."

"Take it easy. Slow."

A grating rasp of metal as Shefflin pried. The padlock parted with a snap. Keno turned the lamp flame far down and pulled open the door. Shefflin had grabbed Vedder under the arms, and now he backed in, tugging the gunman with him.

"Rapped him a good 'un. He won't trouble a spell."

"We'll tie him anyway," Keno muttered. "Garfield, tear a blanket to strips. How'd you know?"

"Warn't no trick. My shanty's just one over. Ole Bone is got long ears. Heerd most o' it, guessed some. Then waited a spell. Let's go get that there gold, cousin."

Keno bent and yanked Vedder's Colt from its holster. He straightened up, facing Shefflin, before he answered.

"No gold." His voice was quiet and hard. "Now we'll be lucky to clear off this roost alive."

Shefflin's avid stare turned wild. "You made a bargain. Now I done right by you and you're a-breaking it."

"Use your head. Baffin's at the gate. We can't

even get past him without raising the whole camp. If we did and had a third-ton of gold bullion loaded muleback, how far you reckon we'd get?"

"You got something in your craw though, boy," Hook grunted. "I know that look. Spill it."

Keno nodded, smiling a little. "Just an idea. Maybe we save our necks and get out of here and have a tidy profit, all together. Listen."

CHAPTER NINE

People tripped themselves up on too-elaborate schemes. That was what had been amiss with Pop's plan, Keno said. There had been too many ways for something to go wrong. Keno could be as devious as the next man if the situation demanded, but his own plan was shorn of complications and straightforward as a bullet.

Hook liked it and said so. Shefflin looked a bit uneasy, but he agreed. The whole idea, though, was too simple for Garfield, who felt more comfortable with indirectness—and less direct risk. Maybe they'd do better to settle for getting out past the guard and forgetting the rest. Did he want out of the money, then? Not at all, Garfield answered sulkily; if they were determined to go through with it, he might as well cut his share of the pie.

"All right." Keno knelt on the floor and motioned Garfield to kneel beside him. He thumbed a cartridge out of his belt and handed it to the con man. "Want you to draw a floor plan of Westerman's house. Doors and windows in particular."

Garfield did so, using the blunt-nosed slug to sketch a diagram on the packed-clay floor. Keno noted how the sleeping area was ranged along the rear of the building. Garfield's bedroom was at the southeast corner, Luana's at the southwest, the Major's between them. All three rooms opened on one narrow corridor. A window pierced each outside wall of Garfield's room.

"We don't go in by the parlor," Keno said. "Noticed last night those boards creak. You say Hessie's got a bunk in the kitchen, so we don't go in that way." He stabbed a finger at the broken line indicating the west window of Garfield's room. "We go in here. It's a hop-skip to the other rooms. Once we got them two, it don't matter what sort of a row is raised. "We're good as out."

Leaving Vedder trussed like a Christmas goose, they doused the light and slipped from the shanty. Between them and the Westerman cabin lay an open stretch of compound whitened by a full glare of moonlight. From his position at the gatehouse two hundred feet away, Baffin could easily spot them as they crossed it. If he weren't dozing and if he chanced to be looking that way. But Baffin had spent many such nights on long boring watches, and Keno was willing to gamble that by now his alertness had slacked till he was either napping or negligent.

"We'll go across one at a time," he whispered. "Go like you was going over eggs. Don't make a sound and don't run. Don't dawdle either."

"Baffin is got a big old Sharps," Shefflin said hoarsely. "Dead shot too. If he sees one o' us, he will bust him wide open."

"Hell," Hook growled, "let's quit talking. I'll go first."

"Cover your hook," Keno murmured. "Moon hits on it like a mirror."

Hook shoved the bright steel in his coat pocket and then, ducking low, moved across the open area like a swift shadow. Despite his squat bulk, he covered the distance with a lightfooted grace and in complete silence. Garfield went next. He bounded like a scared antelope and managed to send a few pebbles skittering noisily over the gravelly ground. Keno waited for a few aching seconds after Garfield had achieved the other side. When nothing happened, he jabbed Shefflin's arm to start him moving. The wolfer went across at an ungainly shuffle, but he made no sound. Keno made his run and came up to the others where they stood flattened against the cabin wall.

As Garfield had said, the window was fitted into its frame from the outside, a couple of nails tapped in to secure it in place. Keno used a jackknife he had taken off Vedder to work the nails loose, whittling away the wood around their square shanks till he could pry them out of the frame. This took a good ten minutes. Afterward he lifted out the frame and set it on the ground. Then he and Hook pulled off their boots.

"Shefflin, get to the east wall. Keep a watch from there. Garfield, watch this side."

The window was high and narrow. Keno thrust his shoulders and torso through and then maneuvered a leg over the sill and lowered himself carefully to the floor. Entrance was more difficult for Hook, but with Keno's help he made it. Moonlight filtered the room's details into dim relief. Keno picked out the outline of a door, the bed, and the commode with a lamp on it. His sock feet whispered across the floor; he raised the lamp's chimney, produced one of the matches he had found in Vedder's pocket, and lighted the wick, afterward turning the flame far down.

Handing the lamp to Hook, he pulled Vedder's gun from his belt, catfooted to the door, and softly raised the latch. Hook was at his heels as he went into the corridor. The dim spoon of flame threw a weird blur of gray shadows along the log walls. Keno halted by the adjoining door and with infinite care lifted its latch. He pushed open the door suddenly and went in, his gun leveled.

Westerman didn't wake. Keno moved to his bedside and held the gun a few inches from his head and cocked it. The Major groaned and harrumphed his way out of a dead sleep. Then his eyes blinked wide.

"You're a fool." In an utterly flat tone.

"That'll turn out only if you've lost your fancy for living, Major. In that case, you're a bigger fool."

Westerman didn't reply.

"Hook, set down that lamp and toss his clothes over."

Hook went to the cane-backed chair where the Major's clothes were neatly draped. He placed the lamp on its seat and rifled through the Major's shirt, coat and trousers before throwing each garment on the bed. He turned up a Derringer from an inside pocket of the coat.

"Look at that," he muttered. "Made to hold a shotgun shell."

"Watch him," Keno said.

Going to the Major's commode, he lighted the lamp on it and, holding it in his left hand, went out of the room and down to Luana's doorway. The door was slightly ajar. Keno nudged it open with his foot and went in noiselessly.

She was sleeping so lightly that she came awake at once and sat up.

"Don't make a row, miss. We're going out of this place and you and your pa are going with us."

She pulled the bedclothes up to her throat. "With Giles—or whatever his name is?" Her eyes were reddened, as if she had cried herself to sleep. So her father had told her.

"Yeah. Him too. You'll need some riding duds."

"If you think—!"

"I'll turn my back, lady. But you stay where you

are. You just might have a gun hid somewheres. I'll fetch what you need."

He set the lamp down and went to the tall armoire in one corner. Opening it, he found among the layers of fancy dresses a fashionable new riding outfit with one of the divided skirts that until recently had been seen only on circus equestriennes. Keno carried the outfit to the bed.

"I'll need some—er, linen—"

She blushed angrily as she spoke, more taken aback by the impropriety of the situation than by its danger. Actually her fully flowing nightgown covered her fully, even if the drawn-up covers didn't. Keno almost smiled. A girl like her was as totally alien to his experience as having a man in her room was to Luana Westerman's.

"You'll have to name what you want, ma'am."

She did, blushing even more furiously as she directed him to the second bureau drawer. He kept his face poker straight as he handed her the dainty things and then walked to the corner and stood facing the armoire.

"Suppose," she said coldly to his back, "that I don't care to oblige you."

"You got about one minute to decide that you will, ma'am. That's all I can spare you."

He didn't elaborate, but the hint was enough. After a long, painful pause, he heard her quick movements. He stood patiently and counted off the seconds in his head. Listening to her slightly frantic struggle with her clothing, he said, "That's one minute, ma'am. Two more." He had only a brushing acquaintance with the mysterious cinches and latigos of feminine attire, but that little let him sympathetically extend the time.

He nearly turned his head when a floorboard lightly groaned in the corridor. But he could not glance at the doorway without looking toward the girl, and it sounded like a normal creaking of house timbers.

So he thought. Then Hessie said crisply, "Don't you turn, mister. Put your hands high."

Keno turned his head slowly. The maid stood in the doorway, her gaunt figure straight in the sack-like folds of her woolen nightdress. She held a long Greener shotgun leveled at him.

The words were hardly out of her mouth when Hook glided into view behind her. He snaked his good arm quickly around her, grabbed the shotgun barrel and twisted it upward. She screamed, jerking both triggers at once. The Greener exploded its two loads into the ceiling.

Hessie struggled wildly to free the shotgun from Hook's grasp. His metal member made a steel-winking arc as he rapped the hook's blunt curve against her temple. As she went limp, Hook caught her and eased her down.

Keno was already springing past them through the doorway. Three steps brought him to the Major's doorway just as Westerman, clawing wildly through a commode drawer, came out with a snub-nosed pistol.

Keno fired into the commode, placing his shot within three inches of the Major's up-whipping arm. Westerman froze in place. He was half-turned away, the little nickel-plated gun poised above the drawers. His eyes glared; his mustaches bristled. He couldn't complete his turn and bring the pistol around before Keno fired again. Opening his hand, he let the gun clatter into the drawer.

He was fully dressed except for his coat. Keno got it and chucked it at him, saying flatly, "Into the hall."

He prodded Westerman ahead of him to his daughter's room. Luana was on her knees holding the maid's head in her lap, sobbing. "You brute! Oh you brute! Poor Hessie—"

"Greener went off like a young cannon," Hook growled. "Whole camp'll be on our necks directly."

Keno strode to a window and poked the curtain aside with his gun barrel, peering out across the dark compound. He saw lamplight flare in the bunkhouse windows. "Roused 'em, all right."

He came back to Westerman and jammed the gun into his belly. "Major, listen hard. I won't say it twice. There's four of us going out that gate, and you and your girl're going with us."

Westerman's mustaches quivered. "Like hell we are."

"We're going out front now—just you and me— and you're going to tell that hardrock crew of yours to give us a wide berth. More particular, you're going to tell Baffin and his cockroaches the same thing. Hook, keep the two women here. If there's shooting, no sense them being in line. When I hooraw you, bring the girl out." He jammed the gun harder. "All right, Major..."

"By God, you'll swing for this," Westerman said in a cold fury. "I promise you!"

"Take it that means you're about to do as told."

For answer, Westerman turned on his heel and strode to the doorway. Keno murmured, "Slow," and followed him with lamp and gun.

They passed through the parlor and came out on the porch. Men's voices were raised in sleepy complaint as they came pouring out of the bunkhouse. "What'n hell's up?" a man yelled. "Someone's after the gold sure," said someone else. That opinion seemed the general consensus, for in the smoky light of the bobbing lanterns carried by several, Keno saw saffron glints of gunsteel: they were armed almost to a man.

"All right, Garfield—Shefflin," Keno said dryly. "You can come out. I got our passport in hand. Bring our boots."

The con man and the wolfer came warily out of

the shadows from opposite flanks of the cabin. They moved up beside the two.

"What'n hell was that shooting?" Shefflin demanded. Garfield said nothing, but Keno could actually hear his teeth chattering.

"Shotgun went off. Nobody hurt." Keno kept his eyes on the muttering body of men, and when he, saw them starting to converge in his direction, nudged Westerman's ribs with the Colt muzzle. "Tell 'em, Major."

"Men," Westerman called hoarsely. "I want you to stop. Stay where you are."

The whole gang milled to an uncertain halt about a hundred feet off. Roddy Baffin was among those in the lead, and both Rudirosa and Jubilo were close beside him.

"You want six horses saddled and brought here," Keno said. "Mine, Hook's, Garfield's, and Shefflin's —yours and your girl's. Tell 'em!"

Westerman chokingly gave the order.

"Major, what'n hell anyhow?" a man shouted. "That there's the insurance feller with a gun agin your—"

"He ain't no insurance man, you dumb rummy!" Baffin snapped. "He's after the gold—or was. What's your game now, Mr. Landry?"

"It don't need to concern you," Keno said. "All you got to do is stand aside and keep your guns leathered while we-all ride out. Major 'pears to want it that way."

There was an outbreak of angry muttering. The men seemed to waver. They looked raw-eyed and dangerous in the muddy play of lantern light.

"Dammit, do like he tells you!" Westerman said. "There's a gun on me and another on my girl inside. It's our lives, don't you understand? They got nothing to lose. Baffin!"

"All right, Major, if that's the order." Baffin wheeled to face the miners; Rudirosa and Jubilo ranged out beside him. "You and you and you"—he pointed at several different men—"go fetch them horses like he said. Rest of you buckos break up there, get back by the bunkhouse."

With sullen grumblings, they slowly obeyed. *That's it*, Keno thought, the fist of pressure unknotting in his chest. They were as good as out, unless some itchy-fingered character blew the situation wide open. It would take just one shot. He could have added an order for them to discard their guns, but that would be crowding luck with a crew of tough nuts like this one.

When he saw the men coming with the horses, Keno called to Hook. He came out to the porch with Luana. Against the night cold, she wore a bonnet and a heavy dark traveling cloak that muffled her neck to foot.

"Hello, Giles," she said icily.

She had a wintry self-possession about her now. Garfield, on the other hand, looked a nervous wreck.

"Left the colored gal hogtied," Hook said. "She's all right. Won't get but a big headache out of it."

He and Keno sat down to tug on their boots. Afterward Keno moved Westerman over to the horses. "Mount up, Major. And listen: you got any bright ideas, I'd get rid of 'em. Remember. It's her neck too." He lifted his voice. "Baffin!"

"Yeah, bucko."

"Go ahead of us and open the gate."

"Just as you say, bucko."

Keno lifted his catch rope from the saddle and ran a lead line from Westerman's bridle to his own saddle horn. Hook did the same for Luana. "We'll ride out first," Keno said. "Shefflin, bring up the rear with Garfield."

They rode in a slow cavalcade toward the gate. The men had pulled to either side, forming a broad alley. Some of the steam had run out of them, seeing that Keno and his companions had no apparent designs on the gold. Few, if any, gave a tiny damn about Westerman's neck, Keno guessed, but few were without some concern for Miss Luana's. That was as solid a reason as any for putting plenty of distance between themselves and here and making sure that nobody would follow.

Baffin stood by the gate which he had swung open. Keno halted his horse and looked at the gunman. "I'll say it slow so it sinks in. Stay here all of you. Don't follow us and don't send anybody after the law. You won't do these two any good."

Baffin nodded lazily. "And what happens to 'em if we do like you say?"

"Then nobody gets hurt. What do you say, Major?"

"Do as he tells you." Westerman said the words as if he were spitting melon seeds. "Don't anyone leave the compound—unless you don't hear from us inside of twenty-four hours. Then I want—"

"That's enough," Keno cut in. "He'll know what to do, all right. But you'll be back here before then. Now move."

The horses went out the gate and began the slow, clattering descent of the stony trail. The stockade was silent behind them. There was no pursuit.

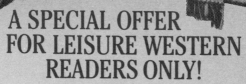

GET YOUR 4 FREE BOOKS NOW— A VALUE BETWEEN $16 AND $20

Mail the Free Book Certificate Today!

FREE BOOKS CERTIFICATE!

YES! I want to subscribe to the Leisure Western Book Club. Please send my 4 FREE BOOKS. Then, each month, I'll receive the four newest Leisure Western Selections to preview FREE for 10 days. If I decide to keep them, I will pay the Special Members Only discounted price of just $3.36 each, a total of $13.44. This saves me between $3 and $6 off the bookstore price. There are no shipping, handling or other charges. There is no minimum number of books I must buy and I may cancel the program at any time. In any case, the 4 FREE BOOKS are mine to keep—at a value of between $17 and $20! Offer valid only in the USA.

Name_____

Address_____

City_____ State_____

Zip_____ Phone_____

Biggest Savings Offer!

For those of you who would like to pay us in advance by check or credit card—we've got an even bigger savings in mind. Interested? Check here. ☐

If under 18, parent or guardian must sign.
Terms, prices and conditions subject to change. Subscription subject to acceptance. Leisure Books reserves the right to reject any order or cancel any subscription.

GET FOUR BOOKS TOTALLY *FREE*—A VALUE BETWEEN $16 AND $20

▼ Tear here and mail your FREE book card today! ▼

PLEASE RUSH
MY FOUR FREE
BOOKS TO ME
RIGHT AWAY!

Leisure Western Book Club
P.O. Box 6613
Edison, NJ 08818-6613

AFFIX
STAMP
HERE

CHAPTER TEN

Keno pushed hard all night to make the foothills. He dismounted and climbed to one of the craggy ridges and inspected their back trail. The desert pancaked away to the northern heights from which they had come; the lowlands were dark undulating shades of maroon in the tawny light. In all the open waste, there was no movement, no sign of life.

Keno descended to where the others waited, slumped in their saddles.

"How's it look?" Hook asked.

"Nobody followed," Keno said. He swung back to his saddle and quartered his animal around till he was facing Westerman. "Here's how it is, Major. Listen good."

Westerman raised his head. He was no longer young; he had gotten soft in recent years. The long night ride had told heavily on him. His face was gray with fatigue, his jaws furred with a silvery stubble.

"Three days from now," Keno said, "Friday noon —got that?—we want to find fifty thousand in good federal currency stashed at the foot of Eagle Rock." He had gotten the name of the small mountain from Shefflin. It stood roughly five miles to the southeast of their present position: a distinctively flat-topped cone that rose out of the lesser foothills like a raw knuckle. "There's a lone dead tree at the foot of the eastern base, the wolfer tells me. You—or somebody, don't matter how—cache the money directly at the foot of that tree and plant a rock on it. Then you or the Mister Somebody get your tail the hell back to your roost. Miss Luana will show up there before sunset. My word on it..."

"Your word!" Westerman spat.

"Most people call it good," Keno said imperturbably. "You got no choice, old man. Just a word of advice. I wouldn't send any men out after us, I was you. Not till your daughter has got back safe."

"If she is harmed," Westerman whispered, "in the least way—"

"She won't be. No chance of it unless you're fool enough to send a passel of gunnies instead of the money. If lead got flying, anyone could get hurt, her included. You won't take that chance, Major."

Westerman clenched the fingers of one hand over his pommel, squeezing till the veins stood out. "I'll need time to lay my hands on that much cash."

"Three days is time aplenty for a man of your means. You better tie to this, Major. We ain't waiting. Friday noon we find the money there and Miss Luana goes free. Or it ain't and she rides out of this valley with us."

Westerman nodded jerkily. He turned those frosty eyes on Garfield. "I never liked you, boy, but I never had cause to doubt you, either. When you leave the valley, just don't stop. Don't stop for a long, long time, boy. Always watch your back and don't ever feel safe in your guts. There'll be detectives on your trail. They'll stay on it long as my money holds out. My word on it." His glance shuttled to Keno. "As for you—"

"Get going," Keno said flatly.

Westerman looked at his daughter. He cleared

his throat and shook his head slightly, as if groping for a word, anything that could be his talisman to her.

"Go along, Pa. They won't hurt me."

The Major wheeled his mount, lifting him into a tired trot as he headed up-valley in the sallow dawn.

When he'd dropped out of sight beyond a low ridge, Keno said, "All right, Hook, take the lead."

Hook swung south at a slow lope, and the others fell in behind. Dad Tasker had chosen the site for a rendezvous weeks ago: he and Hook had laid out a carefully circuitous route to it. It was, so Dad had said, a place where they could fort up for months if necessary and not be found.

They rode steadily southward for an hour, Hook making no effort to disguise their trail. At last he plunged into a shallow defile between two scalped hills and then through a forest of chaparral whose thorny fingers tore savagely at their clothing. Breaking free of it, they descended into a narrow and rock-floored ravine and rode it out to a sudden drop-off in a rushing stream. Hook rode his horse confidently into the water and headed upstream, picking his way carefully across the slick round boulders that broke the crystal flow. The stream-banks gradually rose and became frost-pitted limestone ledges. Finally Hook climbed his horse out of the stream, ascending the bank at right angles. He said, "Go slow," and they followed him single file, lunging their horses up onto the bare scorched rock. It was flint-hard; their mounts' hooves left no impression, and the drops of water they showered on the sun-warm limestone quickly faded.

"Not much farther," Hook said. "Rest the horses."

He swung to the ground and walked his animal up and down. The others dismounted too, rubbing their arms and legs as they stretched out the kinks. The men used the respite to shed their coats against the mounting sun; Luana tied her heavy cloak behind her saddle but kept the bonnet on to shield her fair complexion.

Garfield covertly watched her as he walked his horse back and forth. Finally he sidled casually over by her. "Look, my dear, why can't we make the best of things and be, ah, uh, friendly? I mean, we'll be out here for three whole days and nights, and there's no point being cold, if you know what I mean."

As he spoke, Garfield ran his gaze warmly over her slim figure in the tailored riding suit. It was probably the same intimate manner of look and speech by which he had softened her other times, but just now it was ill-chosen.

Luana eyed him expressionlessly. "I'd have to be pretty much of a dunce *not* to know what you mean."

Garfield blinked. "I didn't mean that."

"No, you don't *look* it." She laughed quietly. "But then I've given a fair impression of a dunce all along, haven't I? I must have seemed a terribly easy mark to a man of your, ahem, *experience.*"

Garfield began to redden. "It wasn't like that. I mean, it wasn't all like that. I mean—"

"I know what you *mean.* When I was little, I read tinselly romances where a certain type of male was commonly described as an unspeakable swine. I always wondered just what kind of a man that might be. Well, you've rounded out my education, Giles; I'll give you that. I may even give you a new name. How does U. Swine strike you...?"

"You can't talk to me that way!"

"Of course not," she taunted. "You can always hit me. Why don't you, Giles? Surely that's not beneath you."

"Button it," Keno said. He rose in one motion from the ledge, snapped his cigarette into the water, and walked to his horse. "Let's get moving."

As Hook took the lead again, Keno grinned a little over what he had just witnessed. Probe about one inch below Luana Westerman's velvet surface and you hit a spirit like carbonized steel. He had seen from the first that in some ways, in spite of Garfield's being the silver-tongued con man and she his innocent victim, hers was the dominant personality in their relationship. By her own admission she thought of him as "a little boy." Keno would have simply said that Garfield's behavior was in some respects clumsy, eccentric, and foolish; but Luana, being a woman (and vulnerable to that degree) put a maternal—which was to say dominating—interpretation on his foolishness. Maybe the interpretation was justified. She'd dressed him down and sewed back his ears with a neat, precise needle, and Garfield had flared up like a sullen little boy.

They were climbing into the foothills now, rounding spirally up a slow-rising base of giant peak. They had held to rocky, bare terrain since leaving the stream, and Keno knew that the best tracker would have a near-impossible time picking them up now. He saw no sign of a trail on the flinty flank of mountainside, yet Hook chose his way upward with an almost careless ease, now walking his horse along a narrow ledge, again lunging the animal up a sharp incline. The higher they went, the more treacherous the going was. They rode single file most of the time, Garfield and Shefflin following Hook, Luana behind them, and Keno bringing up the rear.

They achieved a flat granite ledge and followed its curve around the slope till it terminated in what appeared to be a black fissure that deeply split the solid rock, running back a few yards and then pinching off completely.

Hook rode straight into the cleft, cramping his shoulders as they brushed the uptapering walls.

Then, as he seemed about to collide with its vee-shaped terminus, he swung his mount hard to his right and momentarily vanished from view. Moving after him at a gingerly pace, the others found themselves turning at right angles down a short tunnel. It ended in a blaze of daylight.

They had come out into a kind of long, narrow cove, which was really a deep gorge that gashed the lower edge of the mountain flank at this point. It was cut off from the outside by a vast shelf of rock that must have broken from the rim long ago, falling into the gorge's bottleneck end and wedging itself flush with the mountain's soaring flank. Over the years debris had filled the cracks between; weather had stained the flat wedge to the hue of the surrounding rock. Now, from the outside, it looked like the original mountainside, totally disguising the gorge, at least from below. Only the slender fissure that Dad had found by accident offered entrance to this end of the gorge.

The stream that had carved the gorge out apparently came from a subterranean channel at the gorge's far upper end. It gushed down the full length of the slanting canyon floor and out beneath the blocking wedge down toward the lowlands. This, Keno guessed, was the origin of the creek they had followed earlier.

A broad ledge had been worn out of the softer rock some yards above the water. It was a good twenty feet wide, nearly a hundred feet long, and littered with chunks of fallaway rock from the rim above. There was a stack of sawed cordwood that had evidently been packed in on horseback, also a strewing of gear, cookpots and grub, and blankets around the ashes of a dead fire. But nobody in sight.

"Quit the games, Dad," Hook said a little irritably as he swung to the ground.

Dad Tasker's squat, dwarflike form edged from behind a huge chunk of crumbled shale. He held his rifle half-ready as he moved toward them, taking everything in with his snapping young-old eyes and obviously not liking what he saw.

"Goddammit, what's this? What's *he* doing here"—jabbing a thumb at Shefflin—"and *her?* Where'n hell's the bullion?"

"You can forget about it," Keno said idly, and stepped from his saddle. He tossed his reins to Hook and then turned to face Dad and peeled off his gloves, watching the rifle Dad held. He knew the old man's immediate reaction would be stark unreasoning rage, and no telling what he might do.

"Forget?"

"We didn't get it out. Too dangerous."

"Dangerous! Goddam you, boy! I planned this for months—beat my ass sore riding these hills to find a hole-up like this'n! I planned it and I worked on it and I set it up! You agreed t'do the job. Now you thrown me over—all you bastards!"

He was tensed to a bundle of quivering sinew, his face twitching and putty-colored. His fists were clenched white-knuckled around his Winchester. Keno, his hands resting lighty on his hips, gave the rifle a pointed nod.

"Before we go on with this," he said gently, "set that on the ground."

Dad's small eyes were points of red flame.

"Do it, Dad."

He didn't raise his voice or change its easy, patient drawl. No need to. Dad Tasker knew his foster son too well to argue. He bent and laid the rifle down.

"One of Westerman's guards, Baffin by name, knew Hook. He told Westerman. We was locked up along with Garfield. Shefflin busted us out for a cut of the pie. That's why he's along."

Unmollified, Dad nodded jerkily toward the girl, snapping, "Why's she?"

"She's Westerman's daughter."

It was comical to watch all the rage drain from Dad's face, which ran a gamut of expressions from disbelief to awe. "His *daughter?* Westerman's?"

Dad turned away, combing his fingers through his dirty white mane. Then he swung back, staring at Keno, his scarred face twitching more violently than before. "I be damned," he whispered.

"See it now?"

"How much?" A fevered laugh racked Dad's flinty mouth. "What we getting for her, boy?"

"Fifty thousand."

Dad stared at him. "Fifty—? Hell's fire! You could of stuck him for the goddam quarter million that gold is worth! Hell, more!"

"Man trips himself up getting too fancy and too greedy. That's been your trouble. Fifty thousand will pinch Westerman without squeezing him."

"But goddammit! I want him squeezed! Squeezed and bled dry!"

"That's your problem," Keno said coldly. "All I'm concerned with, if we soak him too much he might feel crowded enough to run a sandy, trick us some way. But I don't reckon he'll risk her life to keep from handing over fifty thousand. Another thing, he can round up that much cash in three days' time, which is what I give him. And cash is what we want."

"I had a buyer set up for the gold!"

"Sure. But we'd of had to lay low here a long spell till it was safe to move the gold out of the valley. Westerman'd have these hills swarming with men on the hunt for us."

"Hell! They'd never of found this—"

"Why in hell not? You found it, didn't you? This way we just pick up a fat bag of cash—noon Friday at Eagle Rock—take the girl with us a ways, then let her go and split for the border."

Dad subsided, mumbling. Keno glanced about at the disorder and litter of the bivouac. "All right, let's offsaddle, clean up this rat's nest, and set up camp."

The others dropped wearily out of their saddles, Hook stepping around his horse to give Luana Westerman a hand down. As she dismounted, the divided skirt curved smoothly against her hip and thigh. Garfield stood fingering his reins and watching her with a mingled frustration and anger.

Nor was he the only interested party. Bone Shefflin was covertly following her with his eyes. Dad Tasker too was giving her an oddly intense stare that had nothing to do with lust. Something more personal, Keno guessed. Dad hated Westerman, and she was his daughter.

Three days, Keno thought.

That should be more than enough time for a lone girl among five men to brew up a situation or two. The kind that spelled purely trouble.

CHAPTER ELEVEN

A number of small feeder canyons branched off the gorge, and Dad pointed out one where he had penned his own horse, stretching a couple of ropes across the mouth. While the others set up camp, Keno and Hook watered their animals and then turned them into the corral canyon.

"The old man picked quite a hole-up here, wouldn't you say?" Hook grunted as he lashed one of the holding ropes back to the rock pinnacle that had anchored it.

"About as likely as you could find." Keno was securing the rope's other end. "Has a few drawbacks, though. That stream for example. Anyone found us, the noise would cover his approach. Another thing, we're protected on all sides from being spotted at long or short range, but wide open to anyone on the rim...."

Hook craned his head, studying the gray, crumbled rimrock fifty feet above. "Yeah. And anyone could easy reach it if he worked up around the gorge."

"If anyone discovered that crack we came in by," Keno added, "one man on the outside could keep us from leaving while a rifleman on the rim picked us off. No shelter from above except that crack tunnel; we'd still be pinned."

"Like you say," Hook said. "Maybe we better mount a guard. Say two-hour shifts for each man. I'll take the first watch."

They walked back to the others. Garfield had built a pyre of twigs in the ashes of the old fire; he was about to strike a match. Keno destroyed the pyre with a sweep of his boot.

"No fire till after dark. Do I got to tell you why?"

"You better," Hook said. "He's got a headful of slow savvy, this boy."

Dad hobbled over, dour-faced. "Cooked up a goodly mess of stuff last night." He motioned at a tarp-wrapped bundle. "Beans, beef, pan bread. Help yourselves."

He stumped across to a canvas rucksack set in the shade of a boulder and rummaged in it, pulling out a quart bottle. From the several clinking sounds in the rucksack, he had a good reserve stashed inside. He yanked the cork with his teeth and took a long pull. Bone Shefflin's Adam's apple bobbed sympathetically; he licked his lips.

"Might you spare ole Bone one o' them flasks o' painter sweat, Mr. Tasker? Will sure enough pay you back out o' my cut."

Dad lowered the bottle, eying him surlily. "Suppose I got to or you'll rob me blind while I'm sleeping, you son of a bitch."

Shefflin looked injured. "I would pluperfect-sure pay you back, sir."

"Damn right you will. One. You best make it stretch."

He pulled another bottle from the sack and tossed it over. Shefflin snaked it out of the air, grinning vastly. "Thankee, cousin."

Hook walked to his saddle and pulled his rifle from its scabbard. "I better get to the watch." He glanced at Dad and Shefflin, then at Keno. "I'd say here's where the real watch is needed, boy."

"So would I," Keno said. "Don't worry, they ain't neither of 'em going to get so whiffletreed they can't stand guard."

Hook went to the fissure and vanished inside it. Dad, sitting on the ground a little distance from the others, stared down into the frothing stream, taking quick short nips from the bottle. Keno opened the tarp bundle and helped himself to bread and beef. He built a sandwich and munched it, thoughtfully eying Dad. He had never before seen the old man drink like this. Was he upset about the gold? Hard to tell. He just kept nipping away and staring into the water.

Luana had removed her bonnet and riding jacket. She knelt by her saddlebags, unbuckling the straps of one.

"What're you doing?" Keno said.

"Just getting out a comb, if you don't *mind*."

"Depends." Keno laid down his sandwich, came over and picked up the saddlebags. Opening the flaps of both, he upended them, dumping their contents on the ground. There were a lot of female oddments that made little sense to him. He saw no gun, which was all that concerned him. "Sure enough. There's your comb."

He went back to his sandwich. She glared at him a moment, then began to comb out her light brown hair. It was in a hopeless tangle, for it had been brushed smoothly out before she had retired last night, and she'd had no chance to groom it since. With the comb and quick expert fingers, she curried it out in a silky burnished fall that rippled with coppery lights in the sun. The men watched the way her neck arched, her arms lifted, her easy lovely movements that tightened the once-crisp shirtwaist in little shifting clings across her arms, her shoulders, sketching the points of her small breasts.

She grew uncomfortable under their stares, but stubbornly continued till she had unsnarled the last tangle.

Putting the comb away, she looked at Keno. "I want to bathe."

"Why?"

"I'm filthy, that's why! So are you."

Conceding that this was scarcely debatable, he rose and walked to the steep rocky bank that dropped down to the water. A few hundred feet up the gorge, a thick mass of shrubbery cloaked the entire bank at that point and hung out well over the water. Willow it looked like, with some cottonwood scrub mixed in. The water below back-eddied into a deep, calm pool, as it did at several places along the gorge bottom. Keno dug soap and a towel out of his own gear, gave them to her, and pointed to the thicket.

"There's your dressing room. Get to it."

She climbed down the bank, making her way unevenly along the stony shore to the shrubbery. Shefflin's gaze, whiskey-bright in his slack-lipped face, trailed her.

Dad Tasker was taking deeper pulls at his bottle. His eyes were shiny as jewels and had a faraway look; spots of fevered color burned in his cheeks. He kept chuckling softly to himself. That was another first, Keno thought. A dour grin or a raw ugly laugh was the most he had ever seen from Dad. A chuckle, never.

He looked at Keno. "Westerman's daughter, hey?"

"Said so, didn't I? What's eating at you, Dad?"

"Nothing at all." He cackled a little. "Want a drink?"

"No. You two shove the corks in those bottles, too."

Their stares burned on him. But they did it.

Keno unrolled his blankets in a pocket of rock shade and lay down, tilting his hat over his eyes.

He was starting to feel brittle and edgy, which wasn't the rule with him. But then he'd never undertaken a kidnapping before.

Briefly he considered this. It was a long step up (or down) from the minor excursions he had taken down the shady trail before now. It was even different than stealing the Major's gold would have been, since Westerman was himself robbing the Utes whose land he was mining.

Well, it didn't matter now. The die was cast. He concentrated till he felt his muscles go loose. He dozed in the warm shade....

He heard Luana's thin scream. It brought him to his feet, sweeping a glance around the camp. Dad Tasker was collapsed on his blankets, snoring, literally kayoed by the unaccustomed intake of liquor. No sign of either Garfield or Shefflin....

Keno ran to the edge of the bank. Luana was struggling with Shefflin. Her hair hung in wet strands, though she was fully dressed. He must have ambled drunkenly down there and grabbed her as she was emerging from the thicket after her bath.

Garfield had evidently been dozing too and had noticed Shefflin's absence belatedly, though well ahead of Keno. Anyway he was scrambling across the rocks toward them, and had covered all but fifty of the three hundred feet.

"I'm coming, Luana!" he yelled. "I'm coming—"

This was not very monumental news to Shefflin, who didn't even look around. Garfield reached him and caught his shoulder, trying to pull him away from the girl. The wolfer wheeled with that amazing grace, sweeping out a gaunt arm. He backhanded Garfield across the head so hard he was knocked off his feet.

Keno was already in motion, sprinting down across the rocks. Before he could reach the struggling pair, Shefflin managed one-armed to tear the girl's shirtwaist partly off and pin her like a delicate moth against a sloping rock. The stream's roar covered Keno's approach till he was almost to them. Then it was his long-flung shadow, not any noise he made, that alerted Shefflin.

The wolfer sprang away from the girl and whipped around, his good hand dipping to his boot sheath and flashing up. Keno dived at him before he could pull the blade back to strike, driving his head into Shefflin's midriff like a battering ram. The force of his plunge carried both men backward. They lit in the swirling shallows with a flat-angled splash.

Tussling savagely, they struggled to their knees in two feet of water, Keno's right hand locking Shefflin's knife wrist. Closing with the wolfer for the first time, he became aware of his full bullish power. Shefflin was ambidextrous with his chosen weapon; Keno had to put all his strength into keeping his hold from slipping. He had gripped Shefflin's hurt arm with his left hand; he tried to sip his hold to the broken wrist. But Shefflin's long reach enabled him to keep his wrist beyond Keno's reach.

In the struggle, though, Shefflin rapped the knuckles of his good hand against a rock, causing him to drop the knife. With a roar of bull fury, the wolfer tore his good arm from Keno's grip and grabbed him by the throat, straining him away till he was holding him at the end of his straight arm. Keno was helpless for the moment. Lacking Shefflin's length of arm, he couldn't reach the wolfer's throat—only tug futilely with both hands at Shefflin's straight-held arm.

Shefflin's fingers tightened like steel mandibles. Keno's vision swam, his strength was failing, he could not budge the arm.

Before, he had whipped Shefflin with brains and reflexes. These were his weapons.

He threw his weight backward, at the same time

cramping up his doubled knees between their two bodies. For a moment his head was under water and Shefflin was on top. But it left the uppermost weight topheavy and overbalanced, as he had known it would. Heaving his weight sideways now, he rolled Shefflin into the water, ducking him under. Spluttering, the wolfer relaxed his hold.

A wild upsurge by Shefflin knocked them apart. Keno was the first to flounder to his feet. Shefflin had barely gotten to his knees when Keno lashed out with his boot, slamming the wolfer in the chest and knocking him back into deeper water. Shefflin scrambled partly upright as Keno moved in on him with fist cocked.

The savage momentum of the struggle had carried them toward midcurrent. Suddenly the stream's mild tug was a fierce undertow. They were being swept off their feet, flung together into the main channel, and tumbled like corks down a rock-studded gully of foaming rapids. The two men were slammed against a huge, rounded boulder. Half-stunned, they clung to it in blind reflex. A semicircle of projecting rocks broke the current here. Shefflin used it to drag himself toward shore, crawling from rock to rock.

Keno followed him on hands and knees, over-hauling him just as Shefflin staggered back to his feet. Keno reared up and threw himself on Shefflin's back, driving him to his knees. He clamped on a deadly full nelson, and Shefflin was helpless. Keno applied force, ducking him.

Shefflin tried to surge free, but his thrashing power was immobilized and Keno simply braced his feet and held on. Shefflin's struggles diminished. At last Keno let him go and seized a handful of Shefflin's hair and yanked his head back, holding it above water.

Luana, he saw, had fetched Hook. The one-armed man was scrambling down the bank, his coiled lariat slung over his hook. At water's edge he halted and shook out the coils and, with a little assist from his hook, built a loop one-handed. With one deft snap of his wrist, he sent it twirling end over end across the water as a youngster might spin out a hoop.

Keno caught the noose and passed it over his shoulders and under his arms. Hook drew it tight and then, unable to pull hand over hand, grunted, "Need some help, miss."

With Luana's assistance he hauled the two of them in, Keno dragging Shefflin along. Once they hit the shallows, it was easy to pull the half-drowned wolfer out of the water and fling him face down on the bank.

Hook, as he coiled his rope again, was curious. "How come you didn't let the son of a bitch drown?"

"I'll never know," Keno said. "You got to admit, though, it gives a man something to while away them long winter nights just wondering about."

CHAPTER TWELVE

Keno retrieved Shefflin's knife from the shallow water where it had fallen. He also took the wolfer's pistol. Afterward he went back to camp where Dad Tasker was still snoring off his load and smashed the remaining bottles in the rucksack. That, he knew, had been the cause of the trouble. Unarmed and sober, Shefflin should be no problem.

He expected trouble when Dad learned that his liquor supply had been demolished. But when the old man woke toward sunset and was told, his reaction was a brief sputtering anger, no more. Even that seemed triggered more by the normal irascibility of a hangover than by the destruction of his property, and it passed directly he'd gotten some food under his belt.

Hook finished out his watch and Keno relieved him. Next it was Garfield's turn and finally, as twilight came in, Shefflin's. By then the wolfer had slept off the whiskey and was almost humble.

Keno wasn't concerned about him. It was Dad. At first displeased by the aborting of his scheme to take Westerman's gold, he now seemed downright pleased at the turn of events. He crouched by the fire they had built as dusk came and stared at the flames, occasionally chortling to himself in a secretive and irrational manner.

Keno sat close to the fire himself, for his leather *vaquero*'s outfit was still somewhat damp from the midday soaking, and the night was turning cold. He had dismantled his pistol and cleaned every speck of moisture from the parts. Now, as he reassembled it into the firelight, he covertly studied Dad and wondered. During his boyhood and from time to time over the later years, he'd often had cause to doubt that Dad Tasker was completely sane....

He remembered how as a boy he'd been the frequent target for Dad's explosive bursts of temper. Sometimes the smallest transgression had been enough to provoke them; other times he'd vent his rage for no reason at all. But most of all he remembered that *he* had been the almost unvarying object of Dad's wrath. He had never understood that. Yet bad as Dad would get sometimes, Keno had never seen his hold on reality actually slip. And that seemed to be what was happening. The whiskey had worn off; how else to account for his behavior?

Hook, Garfield, and Luana Westerman were catching up on their sleep. The girl woke and delicately stretched. Then, noting the dropping temperature, she threw her heavy cloak around her shoulders and came to the fire. She had braided her hair and wrapped the braids around her head in a glossy coronet.

"Can't we have a hot meal now?" she asked.

"Sure," Keno said. "Bring some more wood over."

"You really are brimming with gallantry, aren't you?"

"No."

She gave him an imperious stare. "You don't seriously think you're going to get away with this, do you? A kidnapping and extortion—then going scot-free?"

"Right now," Keno said reflectively as he screwed

the butt plates of his revolver back in place, "I can't think of a good reason why not."

He was no Garfield; he couldn't be baited and he couldn't be cowed by her matriarchal manner. Luana forced a little smile. "At least I can thank you for your help this afternoon."

Keno shrugged. "Garfield got there first."

"And got knocked into the middle of next week."

"What'd you expect? Not his fault he ain't a fighter. With me, it's second nature."

"Oh well, I suppose you crooks do stand up for one another. Even worms need a fraternity of sorts."

"I dunno," Keno said idly. "We're mostly honest crooks in this camp. We're all black sheep, I reckon, but leastways the color don't rub off."

"What's that supposed to mean?"

"I mean the kind of fleecing you would of got from Garfield and the kind we're about to give your old man don't amount to shucks next to the grand sort of sneak-thief operation your daddy is bringing off."

"Oh! You have the unmitigated *gall* to compare—"

"No," Keno said coldly. "There ain't no comparison. Garfield would of taken you for a fling and then made off with some of your money. But you'd of been pleasured while it lasted and you'd have got over it fast unless you're a lot less tough than I size you."

"How dare— What a wicked thing to say!"

"Uh-huh," Keno said agreeably. "It's practical, too. So are you. Facts, that's all. You want some more comparisons? The fifty thousand we're getting for you? Man of your daddy's means'll hardly miss it. The gold we would of taken? Hell, your old man was already robbing a lot of dirt-poor Utes of what's rightfully theirs—"

"But those Indians don't care about the gold!"

"That makes it all right, eh? You ever been on

one of the reservations we set aside for the red brethren, Miss Luana? Four times out of five it's a treeless, grassless, gameless piece of burned-out hell the white man can't use. Now. The Grandfather in Washington could send experts to show the Utes how to mine and mill the gold, improve their lot. Not on your tintype, though. It's the same as when Custer found gold on the Sioux lands in the Black Hills. A pack of damned vultures like your old man moved in and set off an Indian war. That won't happen here. These Utes are too beaten down to care. Maybe that makes it all the worse. Maybe someday they'd have learned how that gold could help 'em. Not now, thanks to your daddy."

She was white around the lips, but she didn't reply. Dad Tasker gave a soft, meaningless chuckle. He was watching them both with his bright old lizard's eyes. He looked like a squat gnome in the firelight.

Garfield, wakened by the talk, peered sleepily at them and then groaned out of his blankets. Hook woke too and said he was hungrier than a baby buzzard, and he figured on some fresh-cooked eating. After building up the fire, he prepared beans, beef, pan bread—more of the monotonous fare they had been eating, but steaming hot anyway. Keno carried a plate out to Shefflin.

Afterward Luana said she would wash the dishes and asked for help in carrying them down to the stream. Garfield quickly volunteered, and the two gathered up the pans and plates and vanished below the stony rim of cutbank. Dad Tasker began to prowl restlessly, muttering to himself. Keno and Hook remained by the fire.

Hook gave Dad a thoughtful nod. "You notice it too?"

Keno nodded. "We better keep an eye on him. This a regular thing with him lately?"

"Nope. Oh, he gets some oddments on the brain

now and then, but you know he always did. This's worse'n I seen him."

Keno was silent a moment. Then: "You know just what that old grudge of his against Westerman was? He ever mention it?"

"Not to me."

Hook snagged a chunk of cordwood by impaling it with his hookpoint. He gave a deft flip that sent it crashing on the red-coaled fire, sending up a flurry of sparks.

"Any plans, boy? After we get the money, that is?"

Keno lay back propped on his elbows, chewing on a splinter as he stared at the fresh leap of flames. "Some. Got a Mexican friend in Sonora has a nice piece of land and a horse and cattle operation he wants to sell. Had my eye on it, but no cash."

"You settling in one place? Hard to believe."

Keno shrugged. "Never had a home I can remember. Like to try out the feel once."

"Yeh. Never had one neither." Hook's ugly face was relaxed in thought. "Them brown gals down there're the only women ever looked at this mean pan o' mine and never went into conniptions. Been a moving man all my life, but I ain't getting no younger or no faster. Wonder if I could hunt me up a nice chunky *señorita* and quiet down."

"I'd try it."

"Reckon we could drift down there together?"

"No reason why not." Keno grinned at him. "Want to go halves with me on them horses and cattle?" He was sure Hook was working around to this, but couldn't quite say it out. "We could throw together twice as good an outfit, expand too."

"Damn right," Hook said. They gripped hands; it was settled that simply.

There were a lot of details to hash out, and they had their conversational teeth deep in the subject when Garfield came back to the fire, his arms piled with pans and dishes. A loose cylinder of cordwood was directly in his path, and Keno and Hook quit talking and watched to see if he would. He did. Planted his heels square on the chunk, which shot away from under his boot. Garfield plunged forward, landing on the pans with a tinny crash.

Hook looked soberly at Keno. "He tripped."

Garfield crawled to his knees, gingerly wiped his bleeding nose on his handkerchief, glared at Hook, and began picking up the pans.

Luana came up the bank, carrying a few last plates in her left hand. She set them on the ground by the fire, then moved off several paces and swiftly parted her traveling cloak with her right hand. She had kept it under the heavy folds, and Keno saw that it held a small .32 Colt.

"Don't move," she said coldly. "I know how to use this."

"That's a caution," Keno said, idling to his feet while keeping an eye on the gun. He had noticed something. Before he could make his move, though, she glanced down—"Oh"—and quickly cocked the little pistol.

"Glad you know how to use it," Keno said.

She took another step backward, touching her tongue to her lips. "All right! I don't know much about guns, but I can pull a trigger. And I will if you come any closer—"

"I wonder if you would."

"I will! Unless you do as I say. I want you to throw your guns on the ground, then saddle my horse—"

"What about Shefflin?" Keno said imperturbably. "You got your back to the exit."

She quickly turned her head, then looked back at him. "Don't try to confuse me! It won't work."

"It's already working," Keno murmured.

Hook lounged to his feet now, his ugly face compassionate. "Put the gun down, miss. You ain't going to use it, and if you try to, someone's gonna get hurt."

"That, sir, is the idea! Don't move again—"

Hook sighed and looked at Keno. "Let's get apart a little, boy."

"Good idea."

The two men sidestepped slowly away from each other till they stood a good dozen feet apart. Luana backed up a little farther, her face set and pinched. She brought up her left hand to help steady the pistol. Garfield crouched by the fire as if frozen in place.

"Move in," Keno murmured. He and Hook took a small, measured step apiece, coming closer to the girl.

"Don't!"

The gun clamped in her hands wobbled from one man to the other. Even if she could pull the trigger (and Keno didn't doubt she was capable of doing so) she couldn't take out one of them without giving the other a chance to reach her. She was uncertain, badly rattled too, and Keno thought, *Get to her fast*. A gun in the hands of an amateur could be more dangerous than one held by an expert—and that went double for one held by a nervous woman.

He made a faint, brusque gesture with his left hand, hoping Hook would read it correctly. He did, taking one long step toward the girl. She swung the pistol to bear fully on him and he halted, arms raised.

Keno moved in the same instant that all her attention went to Hook. He launched himself like an uncoiling spring, two straining strides carrying him half the distance to the girl, and then he dove at her.

Her head pivoted; she whipped the gun round in a quarter arc—too far—and swung back. She fired. Keno, coming in just under her line of fire, was so close he felt the powder scour his brow. He heard

Hook's explosive grunt. Then he piled into Luana and dropped her hard, twisting the gun from her hands.

He straightened up and around. "Hook?"

The one-armed man was sprawled on his side, his face set in an agonized grimace as he clamped both hands around his right leg below the groin. The firelight glistened on the wet darkness soaking his trousers.

"Better get out your knife, boy," he said between his teeth. "Cut these pants open."

Shefflin came rushing into the cove. "What'n pluperfect hell?"

"Get back on watch," Keno said calmly as he knelt by Hook and took out his jackknife. He ripped the pantleg up the side till the wound was exposed, then unbuckled and pulled free Hook's broad leather belt. Wrapped twice around his thigh, re-buckled, tightened with a stick twisting the leather, it made a fair enough tourniquet.

Grimacing, Hook grunted himself up on his elbows and studied the wound. "Mop off some o' that blood, boy. Let's have a good look at 'er."

"She ain't pumping anyways," Keno said. "Didn't hit an artery. Would have to burn you then."

"I been burned before. She didn't go through. You gonna have to dig for her, boy. Wisht now you hadn't a' busted all them whiskeys."

"So do I."

Keno stood up, his hard stare pouncing on Luana Westerman, who sat where she had fallen, one hand pressed to her lips. "You help." He strode to his warbag and yanked out a pair of clean shirts and tossed them to her. "Tear 'em up. Long strips. Garfield, stoke up that fire. Dad—fetch a pan of water. Shefflin, I told you to get back on watch. *Do it.*"

He cleaned off the jackknife's large blade as well as he could, then raked a small heap of crumbling coals out of the central blaze and stuck the knife upright in them.

Standing again, he pulled the pistol from his pocket and juggled it in his palm, circling their faces with his eyes. "Never seen this before. Whose is it?"

Garfield, his jaw lopsidedly swollen from Shefflin's blow, swallowed with difficulty. "Er, ah, huh huh, well—"

"Yours. How'd she get it?"

"I, uh, was cleaning it this afternoon, you see, sitting down on the bank in the sun, and, huh huh, I guess I forgot and left it on a rock there."

Keno controlled himself with an effort. "How in hell could you do that?"

"I didn't do it on purpose! Haven't you ever mislaid something?"

"Not my brains," Keno said coldly, "and not a loaded gun around a loose prisoner. You better pray Hook pulls through this on both feet, Garfield. If he don't, you're going to be the sorriest dude alive. Provided you still are, when I'm done."

"You, you, you'd *hurt* me?"

Keno nodded grimly. "On purpose, too."

CHAPTER THIRTEEN

The two days that followed were the most trying of
Keno's young life. Shefflin was untrustworthy, Garfield a blundering incompetent, and Dad Tasker
gradually cracking up. He could trust nobody except Hook, and Hook was in too bad a way to be of
much help. His leg swelled; an old malarial fever
started up and shook him with recurrent attacks.

If he were well, there'd have been no problem.
The two of them could have simply split the
watches; one could sleep while the other kept a
weather eye on their companions. As it was, Keno
had to handle the burden of watchfulness. He collected all the weapons in camp and hid them. His
eyes burned for sleep; he drank gallons of coffee to
keep himself in a semblance of wakefulness, and his
temper turned bone-lean and fierce. Hook lent what
help he could, rousing himself to a weak conscious-
ness now and then, staying that way while Keno
caught forty winks. But the fever and pain would
sweep back, and he'd have to wake Keno before it
wholly engulfed him.

Things hadn't improved by morning of the third
day. Keno found a solitary gray relief in the fact
that the waiting was over. Today they would pick

up the money and be on their way south. And even this was a wellspring of worry for him.

Unwrapping Hook's thigh to change the bandage, he felt sick at the sight. He had feared yesterday that the wound had become infected. Now he was sure.

Propping himself on his elbows, Hook studied the limb with eyes glossed by fever. "How you read it, boy?"

"I seen worse."

"Sure," Hook said softly, wryly, "but any worse'n this and she comes off. And she'll get a sight worse, way it's been going." He paused. "You gonna have to leave me behind, boy."

"No." Flat, brief, positive.

Hook sighed and shut his eyes. "Know better'n to argue. Damn muleheaded young fool...."

Luana came over and sat down on her heels, frowning at the leg, then lifting an angry gaze to Keno. "He can't ride like this. You can't make him! You'll kill him!"

He gave her a chill, bitter stare. "You tell me what, then."

"Leave him here. Go get your—your damned money and turn me loose. I'll fetch a doctor back here."

Keno's hard stare didn't relax.

"For heaven's sake!" she burst out. "Don't you believe me? Don't you understand? You take the money and ride out of the country—free! I'll see that he's taken care of!"

"So will the law," Keno said atonally.

"Won't you take my word not to tell the sheriff?"

"Even if I did, there's the doctor. He'll tell, and your old man'll see that Hook hangs. Or spends the rest of his life in prison, which is a sight worse. No. There ain't but two ways. Neither of 'em's any good, but between leaving him to die sure and taking him along on a slim chance, it's a pretty open choice."

Luana bit her lip. "There's a third way—if you'll trust me. I could bring the doctor here and he could do whatever is necessary. Then you could keep us both prisoner till Mr. Hook is well. Of course you'd probably have to forfeit the money, but if I can forfeit freedom a few more days, then surely—"

Keno cut her off with an impatient chop of his hand. "Use your head. If you ain't back today, your pa will have these hills swarming with men by tomorrow. Sooner or later they'll find this place, and it'll be u. p. with all of us. No. We go ahead as planned."

It was a matter of minutes to throw their gear together and lash it to their horses. Keno returned guns and knives to their owners. With Garfield's help, he lifted Hook into his saddle. Once he was firmly seated, his good leg in stirrup, Hook clamped his big fist over the pommel and said, "Put a lead rope on, boy, and let 'er tear. I'll ride it out."

Keno, seeing the dead sweaty pallor of his face in the shadow of his hatbrim, guessed at the pain caused Hook by the simple effort of holding his saddle. "Feel yourself slipping, don't be proud. Say so. We'll stop."

"Sure, boy. Promise me one thing."

"Depends."

Hook pulled himself erect and let go the pommel to close his sinewy hand on Keno's shoulder. "If it turns out this leg o' mine can't be saved, don't let no sawbones take it off. If I ain't fitten to pull a trigger, you—"

"No."

"God, boy. This he-coon's out an arm now. Take a leg offen him to boot and he won't be a man no more. He won't be but a goddam medicine sideshow."

"You ain't going to lose no leg."

They rode one by one out through the fissure, Keno in the lead with Hook's horse strung to his.

He backtracked across the trail by which they had come, knowing it would bring them out southeast of Eagle Rock. The roughness of the terrain and Hook's condition meant that it would take them all morning and longer to reach the rock, so they'd achieve their destination after Westerman or his messenger had left the money cache there....

Keno glanced back often and anxiously at Hook, but the old one-arm was holding his own. His chin was sunk on his chest and his body rocking almost loosely, but his grip on the pommel was tight as death. He was tough as old boot leather, and Keno couldn't guess at how long he might hold on.

Whenever he looked back, Keno also swept an eye across the others. But that worry at least was damped. A man on horseback in rough country had to tend to business. Garfield, a particularly rotten horseman, was focused entirely on staying in his saddle. Shefflin was occupied with his own mount and leading Luana's. Both he and Garfield had useless right hands, too. Dad Tasker hunched in his saddle like a wizened gargoyle.

The sun climbed against the morning's scoured blue, from a mild warmth against their backs at dawn to a dazzling fury that poured against their left sides by noon. As it began a slow dropping arc toward the deep west, they came finally on the long, broiling, rock-strewn plain where Eagle Rock stood like a truncated cone. In spite of his worry, Keno felt a quickening of pulse. *Fifty thousand dollars!*

He saw the lone dead ironwood thrusting like a skeletal finger out of the rubble along the slope's east base and put his horse straight toward it.

"Git along there, cousin!" yelled Bone Shefflin, a slight thick frenzy slurring his voice.

"Shut up," Keno said, not turning his head. "Ride slow and keep your eyes open."

He didn't expect a trap, but precaution was instinct in a man who rode lonely trails. The plain was rolling and open, and the face of the small peak was bare and treeless. The plentiful boulders on every side were too small to hide anyone but a man on his belly, and if there were men there would also be horses that couldn't be concealed. . . .

Keno halted by the skeleton tree and swung down and tramped to the litter of stones at its base. He turned one over and found nothing. Another, and there it was—a flat but bulky pouch. He opened it and thumbed swiftly through the slim packets. Crisp new bills in good federal currency— he made sure of that much, then returned to his mount and tied the pouch to the horn. Afterward he glanced at Luana.

"Your way's north. Get going."

"You hold on." Shefflin heeled his animal over, keeping a grip on the lead rope of the girl's horse. "We best split that take here'n'now."

"Right now all we do is get out of here," Keno said flatly.

"But you ain't even counted the money! Suppose'n the Major is short changed us?"

"Suppose he has?" Keno said dryly. "What you propose to do about it? Send in a complaint?" He walked to the girl's mount and untied the lead rope. "Get going, lady."

"You hold still, missy. You don't go nowhere. Don't you move sudden, boy, or I'll blow your head off before you bat a winker."

Keno moved only his head, slowly turning it till Dad Tasker came into the corner of his eye. While all eyes were on the pouch, the old man had quietly pulled his horse off from the others. Now he was covering them all with his forty-five.

"What is this, Dad? You want all the take?"

"The take, sure," Tasker whispered. "More'n that. A sight more, boy." His eyes burned madly; he gave a dry, fevered cackle. "Whilst you're standing there, boy, why'n't you shake hands with your sister?"

"What the hell you talking about?"

"Her!" Dad Tasker jabbed his gun toward the girl. "Your own flesh and blood kin! Look at her!"

Scowling, Keno glanced up at the girl. She had lost color, he saw, and her wide-eyed glance moved from Dad's face to his.

"You know what he's running off on?"

"I—I'm not sure. But if..." Her voice faltered and trailed.

"Leave me say it, missy. I waited long enough." Dad was savoring each word like a morsel. "You ain't no chance foundling, boy. You're the son of Lewis B. Westerman."

"You're a liar."

"Shut up!" Dad shrilled it like a steam whistle, leaning far forward in his shaking intensity. "You listen! Your name's Weston Westerman. I taken you right out of your daddy's back yard when you was only two. Missy, tell him! Tell him about your baby brother you never seen!"

"I—don't know. How could I?" Luana stared at Keno, her mouth a trembling stain against her white face. "I was scarcely a month old myself when little Westy was kidnapped. But if it's true...!"

"Goddammit, girl, look at his face! Look at his eyes, nose, chin! Same as yours! Same as your pa's! And the Westerman look—that goddam lordly spit-on-you-all look! All you high-mighty Westermans got it the same."

Keno's jaw hardened. He shuttled his glance to Hook, who shook his head wearily, his fevered eyes puzzled. "I dunno, boy. I just dunno if he's pulling a taffy string or not."

"Hell, Hook got the same story I give everyone." Dad grinned like a death's head. "That's how I found you back of a place night I busted the house at Keno."

"Not true," Keno said softly.

"Not a goddam word. I worked for Westerman roughbusting broncs is how it happened. One day I was sicker'n a dog, but that didn't make no never mind to Major Lewis Be-God-Almighty Westerman. Nossir. He wanted a killer hoss busted that morning. Top him or it's your job, he says. I topped him. Lost my seat but got a foot hung in the stirrup. Some fool'd left the gate open. Got dragged off across the prairie. When a couple of waddies finally overhauled us, I was chopped to ribbons and busted to flinders."

The scars on Dad's brown face twisted like pale worms. "The doc fitted me back together someways, but I didn't walk for a year. Westerman...he paid the doctor bill, then told me to clear out. I faded back in the hills a ways and kept a watch on his place. Mainly on his little boy. Had an English nanny Old Lady Westerman brung in. Used to take little Westy for walks. One day they went a ways out in the prairie and I was waiting. Busted a chunk of wood over that English lady's head and grabbed up the boy and didn't quit a-riding till I was deep in Sonora. Laid low there for five years."

"So that's why," Keno murmured. "All the beatings...and the rest of it."

"You see it, boy? Raised you as tough and mean as I knew how. Meant to turn you into the scummiest killer and outlaw the border ever seen—and let Westerman know. Didn't work out like I planned. Not after you beat me up that time and rode away. After that I was dead scared o' what you'd do if you was ever to learn the truth."

"You had a right to be," Keno said softly.

He casually moved his feet, shifting a few inches to one side. Slight as the move was, Dad's pistol followed, lined on his head, and held that way. Dad might be crazy, but he was alert as a cat. *Keep him talking.*

He said idly, "I expect when you met Garfield you seen another way to get at Westerman, eh?"

"Yeah—yeah," Dad whispered, his eyes like hot steel chips. "That was it, boy. A better way all around. Toll you into robbing your old man—and get my fingers on a fortune into the bargain. Once I had the gold, I woulda done away with the three a' you, Hook and Garfield too, then delivered your body to Westerman with a note telling how I fixed everything. Goddam, wouldn't that a' rubbed his face in it, though!"

Keno nodded. "But this now," he murmured. "Better yet, eh?"

"You billy-be-damned right it is, boy. I got both Westerman's kids right square in my hand—and fifty thousand o' his I ain't sneezing at."

"You was just waiting till we'd collected the money"—Keno took another minute sidestep—"and now you'll kill us both, eh? What about the others?"

"Don't you go moving around like that, boy!" Dad shrilled. He rammed his horse forward, the gun trembling in his knotty fist. "Throw that money pouch over!"

Keno moved slowly to his mount and detached the pouch and tossed it to him. He aimed the toss at Dad's head, hoping to disconcert him for an instant, but the old man snatched it out of the air with surprising ease.

"Leave me tell you how it's gonna be, boy...." Face twitching, Dad gigged his horse forward a few more steps.

All he could do, Keno thought, was choose his moment and then gamble all on a fast draw and a snap shot. But a gray taste of hopelessness filled his mouth already. Dad was an expert shot; his eyes were as good as ever. As he had the drop, speed was of no real account. The most he could hope for would be to take Dad with him....

"First I'm gonna bust your arms, one at a time, Keno-boy. Then both knees."

Keno caught Hook's small, weary movement, but was careful not to shift his glance toward the one-armed man. Dad had pushed his horse forward enough so that Hook was barely in the tail of his vision; he was paying Hook virtually no attention. No reason to. Hook was slumped in his saddle, head down, barely conscious it seemed.

"Then I'm gonna whittle little bits 'n' chunks out o' your carcass. I ain't in no hurry, not after nineteen years. Got all the time in the world."

Slowly, slowly, Hook was lifting his good left hand—hidden offside from Dad's view—to his coat pocket and dipping it down.

"Then this pretty sister o' yours...Only ain't gonna kill her. Hell, no." Dad cackled stridently. "But when I deliver what's left o' her back to her ole man, he's gonna wish I had...."

Hook's hand whipped suddenly up and sideways. The little shotshell-rigged Derringer he had taken from Westerman was almost hidden in his big paw. Its spiteful crack shattered Dad's speech. From three yards away, a spray of lead raked Dad's right leg and the whole flank of his animal.

Dad's cry mingled with the horse's scream. The animal reared high, dumping Dad to the ground. Dad rolled to his feet with an incredible agility. He had dropped his gun. He spotted it in the rubble a few yards away, and lunged for it.

Keno could have shot him then, but ran toward the old man instead, intending to grapple him before he could bring up the gun. But Bone Shefflin moved just as quickly, his long left arm sweeping down to his boot sheath.

A sunflash of blade, a dexterous flip of Shefflin's wrist, silvery loops of caracoling steel as the knife whirled through the air.

Dad had reached his gun and started to bend, but

his fingers never closed on it. He straightened, coughing. The knife was buried halfway to the hilt in his chest. His old veined hands fluttered up like brown leaves, then fell away. He toppled into the rocks and sprawled there like any discarded, shriveled, lifeless bundle.

CHAPTER FOURTEEN

Keno stood looking down at the slight, crumpled body, trying to absorb this on top of what Dad had told him. It was too much to make sense of all at once.

While the others looked on faintly stunned, Bone Shefflin laboriously dismounted and tramped over to the body and bent down. Rolling the frail corpse on its back, he set a boot against its chest and yanked his knife free.

"Damn ole crazy," he muttered, wiping the blade off on his breeches. "He near nailed your hide up for fair, cousin."

"I could've reached him," Keno said coldly. "If I hadn't thought so, I had a gun. There was no damned need."

"'Y God, that's some thanks!" Shefflin ambled back to his horse.

"Best this way, boy," Hook husked. "He was way out of his head and dangerous as a rattler."

Luana, recovering, slipped down from her horse and came over to Keno. Hesitantly she laid both hands on his arms. Her eyes glistened; her lips trembled. "Westy...you *are* Westy. There's a baby picture I've seen...I *thought* that somehow I knew you! So did Pa! That's why."

Keno shook his head numbly. "It don't matter."

"Westy, please—"

"It's Keno."

He felt her quiet shudder, and then her hands dropped and she stepped back. "All right, Keno. But think! You're not what you've been—I mean, not *really.*"

"You tell me who I am, lady."

Her eyes brimmed; tears broke across the lashes and streaked her cheeks. "You're Weston, my brother. You're the son of one of the territory's wealthiest men. The son he's spent a fortune trying to find...the son he's never stopped hoping might be alive somewhere."

"That's touching as hell. Will you quit that damned crying?"

Hook's head swung up; he peered with hard bright eyes at Keno. "Boy, don't you use a rough tongue to a woman. I learned you better."

"All I ever had," Keno said softly, "is what you gave me, Hook. All I ever learned, too. From him" —he nodded at Dad Tasker—"nothing but lickings and hard words. Westerman? I don't remember any Westerman. Neither of 'em was ever a father to me."

Hook understood the unspoken meaning. He bobbed his head up and down, very tiredly. "I'm honored, boy. Real honored. But you give ear to what this little lady says. She ain't just talking about who's kin to who. She is talking about a new life for you."

"Yes, oh yes! Don't you see, Wes—Keno? It's as though *none* of what you've been—or done—was ever real! There'll be no charges pressed—for this —and any old charges against you will be dropped."

Keno nodded stonily. "Daddy's money'll see to it, eh?"

"Your father's money, yes. What's so wrong with using money to right a wrong? You've been willing to commit wrong to get it, so why..." Her voice trailed on a softly appalled note. "I shouldn't—I didn't mean..."

"You said it. I'm a crook. Bred to the bone with crookedness. You don't whelp a growed dog over."

"You're not! You're a good man... or you couldn't have spoken to me as you did—the other night. You made me see something about us—Westermans— that I didn't want to admit. But it was true."

"That's fine. Like father, like daughter. But I'm still the honest crook."

"Westy!" A hardness textured her voice; she held her hands out, palms up. "What do you want of us? What do you expect me to say? There must be *something*..."

"There is." Keno pointed at Hook, who had again slumped semiconscious across his horse's withers. "You see that man? Winters when we was all holed up somewheres, he learned me how to cipher and read and spell K-E-N-O. He learned me how to ride and shoot. He showed me the only kindness I ever got from a living soul. He's more'n a friend, more than a father. Understand?"

"Yes," she said slowly. "I think I do. But I'm not asking you to desert your friend."

"Ain't you? Either way, it boils down to that. Suppose I go back with you and leave either one or both of these two to take care of Hook. They'll drop him somewheres first chance—maybe leave him to die."

"I resent that," Garfield muttered.

"Oh, shut up, Giles!" Luana snapped. The moist-eyed girl of a minute ago had disappeared. "I suppose, Westy, you're afraid of what'll happen to him if you bring him back to the Roost."

"Unless I read your old man a country mile

wrong, I'd say Hook's neck'd be stretched in short order."

"Did it occur to you that together we can soften *our* old man out of any such notion?"

"How? With a shotgun? You want to make me a promise on that?"

"I can't do that," Luana said quietly. "Nobody speaks for him. And he's hard—very. There's a good chance we could change his mind, at the least persuade him to settle for a short prison term for your friend—but I can't promise anything for certain."

"That's it then," Keno said grimly. "I don't take any kind of chance with Hook's life, and he ain't spending even one night in some stinking lock-up in his shape. Not while I got anything to say about it."

"I see," she nodded coldly. "Then may I at least take the money back, or will you carry through that old man's idea and rob your own father?"

"That money ain't all his!" Shefflin bawled. His hand inched toward the boot sheath.

Keno swung up his arm like a pointing gun barrel. "You freeze, Bone. You wiggle one more finger and you'll be shy a hand. He looked at the girl. "You can take back my share and Dad Tasker's. Hook?"

"Give her mine too, boy," Hook whispered, not raising his head.

"Ain't noways fair," Shefflin muttered. "You fellers don't want your shares, us as do should split on 'em."

"Shut up," Keno said, "or you'll be shy your share too. Garfield?"

"I, uh, well, ahem—"

"He'll keep his," Keno told the girl. "You take back thirty thousand."

"Of course." Her icy smile. "Thieves' bargain. The honor of an honest crook."

"That's right."

Keno picked up the leather pouch from where Dad had dropped it. He spilled the contents out on a flat table rock and counted out ten thousand apiece for Shefflin and Garfield. He handed them their shares and restored the balance to the pouch.

He carried it to Luana and held it out. She did not look at it. "Please, Westy. Please come home with me."

"Keno, I said. And home's there." He nodded toward the south.

"Luana," Garfield said thickly.

"What, oh honorable one?"

"Nothing," he muttered.

"Take it, " Keno said flatly.

Slowly she lifted the pouch from his hand and, turning, fastened it to her saddle. Keno gave her a hand up. She looked ready to cry again, and he did not want to watch. "Get going!" He brought his palm flat across the horse's hip, and it moved away. With a quick little sob, Luana turned the animal's head and kicked him into a run, heading north across the bare valley floor.

Keno tramped back to Dad's body, staring dismally down at it. "Best you two get going. I mean to bury him."

Shefflin scraped a palm over his jaw. "Ground's all rocky. Take a heap o' time to plant this ole porcupine."

"Sure."

"There's him." The wolfer tilted his gaunt head toward Hook. "That ole one-wing is in pluperfect sorry shape."

Keno lifted his glance to Hook and saw that he was rolling slowly sideways in his saddle. "Hook!"

"Huh!" The one-armed man straightened up laboriously. He looked blearily at Keno. "That you, boy? Can't hardly make out . . . something wrong?"

"We're going to rest a spell, that's all."

Keno walked to his stirrup and helped the sluggishly protesting Hook to dismount. "Can't waste all this time, boy . . . got a lot of track to make."

"We got a burying first. You rest here."

Keno eased him down in the broad bar of shade flung by the dead ironwood. Hook's face was paste-colored, his eyes glazed, and Keno felt a touch of real fear.

Shefflin snorted quietly. "That ole one-wing, he has built his last loop for sure."

"Shut up."

"Cousin, you ain't a-gonna get him a mile less'n you tie him in his saddle. And time you fetched him five miles, you gonna be toting a dead man."

"Nobody's holding you," Keno said flatly. "Either of you."

"For sure." Shefflin stroked his chin. "Only thing, I know these parts like the back o' my hand, but I ain't never been down by the border or south of it. With all this wampum in my poke, I taken a sudden hanker to see that peppergut country. Not 'thout I'm in company with a feller knows the country, though. Would admire to hitch up with you as far as Sonora, you don't object. But not 'thout we raise plenty dust fast. What I want to know, you gonna pack one-wing along?"

"What if I do?"

Shefflin grunted. "You know pluperfect well what if, cousin. Soon's that girl reaches the Roost and tells her pappy the what-for, ole Major's gonna be hell-afire to find you. You being the son 'n' heir, no skin off yours when he finds us. The dude and me, though, we're good's dead. One-wing too."

"That's right," Garfield said excitedly. "It doesn't make sense, Keno! The three of us can get out of this alive—with a good stake! But if we pack Hook along, we'll be overtaken before we're even clear of the valley. Even if he's not done for, Westerman will finish him off when he catches us. What do you gain him—or us—by bringing him?"

Keno was barely listening. The shadow of an idea

had crossed his mind. "Deron's," he muttered. "Just maybe—"

"What's 'at, cousin?"

"Florentino Deron's place," Keno said thoughtfully. "It's not over four miles west of here. If I can get Hook that far—and he gets proper rest and care..."

Shefflin gave a whinneying laugh. "You blowed your gourd, cousin? Deron? That goddam greaser ain't gonna take on nothing that might get his yaller hide salivated."

"Not for you," Keno agreed. "He's owing me, though. You ought to remember."

The wolfer grinned derisively. "Sure he's owing, cousin. Only you ain't gonna collect off no pepperbelly who's that rabbity you c'n see the yaller streak a-running clear from his hair to his heels. 'Nother thing, Major's got some mighty sweet trackers in his employ. Rudirosa, that spick gunnie now, he works ground like an ole coon hound. He gonna sniff you down in short order, you stay in the valley."

"Know a little about that game myself. I can cover."

Shefflin grinned and shook his head. "You ain't a-gonna cut it, boy. You stick with one-wing, they'll get your back in a corner sure." He nodded toward the hills. "If 'tain't Mexico, over there's old Bone's best bet. Ain't a man alive knows them hills like me. Ain't a soul gonna find ole Bone effen he keeps on the move and makes cold camps. So reckon I'll give you boys fare-thee-well and make heap track for there."

Garfield nervously held in his skittish mount. "I—I'd never make it out on my own."

Keno gave him a glance of utter indifference. "Go with Shefflin. It's like he says."

The wolfer showed his big yellow teeth in a grin.

"That's gospel, cousin. Would be proud of your company."

Garfield shook his head violently. "No! You'd wind up shooting me in the back for my share! That's what you're thinking, isn't it?"

Shefflin shook his head sadly. "You pluperfect sure read this child's sign all wrong, cousin. Your funeral."

He swung his rawboned nag away and put him into a slow lope toward the southwest.

"Let me go with you." Garfield looked really scared. "I'll be no trouble, and I'll help any way I can. Please!"

Keno eyed him stonily. "Don't see what you'd gain. Westerman'll have men out combing this end of the valley, same as everywhere. Good chance we'll be found. I got to stick with Hook, but I can point you the quickest way out of the valley. All you do—"

"I—I—I can't," Garfield chattered. "I'm afraid to go alone...all that wild country beyond the valley. I'd never find my way out!"

He was in a total funk, Keno saw disgustedly, and it would be no use talking reason. Silently cursing his own weakness, he said, "All right. You can come along. But listen, Garfield. You got a knack for fouling any nest you squat in, even when you ain't a mind to."

"I'm accident prone," Garfield confessed dismally.

"Never mind what you call it. I got plenty to worry about even without a goddam jinx like you dogging it along. What I'm saying, you foul my nest any more, any way at all, I'll bust you myself. Come on. Start digging."

"With what?"

"Hands!"

Pulling and prying at the rocks with their bare hands, scraping at the exposed clay with the sharp-edged stones, they scooped out a shallow grave.

Keno wrapped Dad's body in Dad's own soogans and laid it in the excavation. They covered it with rubble, then lugged heavy rocks to fill up the hole and keep out scavengers.

The job finished, Keno straightened and stared down at the unmarked grave, feeling nothing at all. There were no words to say. He roused Hook and assisted him to mount.

Hook's movements were mechanical and so sluggish that he might have been dreamwalking. He barely responded to Keno's voice; once mounted, he slumped across the horse's mane. Keno knew that even if he held to a slow walk, Hook would soon fall out of the saddle. He got his catch rope and used it to lash Hook's hands to the horn, also passing it under the horse's barrel to tie his feet together.

He remembered the shallow brook that ran past Deron's layout. If he was right, they could cut due east and transect it about three miles above Deron's. In saddle again, leading Hook's mount, he headed in that direction.

Garfield, still caught up in a paroxysm of relief, began to while away the time with his usual line of aimless prattle. "I thought all along your face was familiar. Luana's brother! So that's why. She showed me that baby picture of you once, and then there's the family resemblance—"

"Garfield, will you for God's sake button it?"

Keno was disgusted with himself. Garfield was a damned nuisance any way you cut him, but what could he do but bring him along? The poor fool was probably right that he would blunder himself into a real jackpot alone. Not that he was a hell of a lot better off this way....

The hills would have offered better refuge than Deron's hovel, but Hook needed a bed and medicine. The hog ranch would be a far more likely place to take him, for Peggott would have a supply of medicines and might even hide a wounded man for a price. But Peggott's was a good ten miles farther on, and even one additional mile could mean the difference between Hook's making it or not.

Keno picked the route carefully, hanging along gravel or solid rock wherever he could, till he was sure that the trail was well covered. When they came in sight of the creek, he chose a way that brought them across stony footing clear to the water's edge. He walked his and Hook's animals slowly into the water, Garfield moving behind, and headed downstream. He was relieved to confirm that, as he had guessed, the water was no more than a foot deep even in midchannel, chuckling over a firm gravel bottom. If only it held like this all the way to Deron's! Much of the area along these banks was sand and clay that would leave plain sign if they had to leave the water....

They rode slowly. Cottonwood shade dappled the swift amber current; wind rustled the leaves and cicadas rasped in the midday heat. Keno's thoughts unwound a little, but when they did, his mind revolved blackly around what he had learned today.

Westerman's son! He didn't know yet how to feel about that. There was nothing about the man that stirred the vaguest memory of loyalty or affection. The Major had strength, but it was arrogant strength, ruthless and crushing. Having his own sort of strength and pride, Keno wondered whether, if he had grown to manhood as Weston Westerman, exposed to all the uses of naked power, he would be any different.

Hell! He didn't know and didn't really care. All that mattered was what a man had become, not what he might have been. He was just—Keno. The sum of all that Dad's meanness and a young lifetime of privation had beaten into him. How could he be any different—live any different? Above all, just now, came Hook Blanding, more of a father to him than either Dad or Westerman.

What if the Major's men found them? *They'll take Hook over my dead body.* And then he wondered if his defiant attitude didn't stem more from reflex than logic. If they did try to take Hook, he couldn't stop them alone. The best he could do was die with him. On the other hand, if he offered himself up as the Major's long-lost son, was it likely that Westerman would estrange that son by an act of retribution against his comrade?

But he remembered what Luana had said: *He's hard—very.* Even she wasn't sure. And the idea of going to Westerman smacked too much of a capitulation, a form of surrender, to set well in Keno's free-living craw. No, what he was doing was natural to him, wise or not....

Late in the afternoon they rounded a bend in the stream, and Deron's 'dobe was perched on the west fifty yards away. The herder was just turning his flock into the paddock. At Keno's hail, he froze in the act of closing the gate. He turned. A look of dread possessed his face even before his glance lit with surprise on the riders coming along the creekbed. Keno swung out of the water and up the shallow bank. Deron's young wife came to the door of their 'dobe. She promptly shared her husband's uneasy look.

Keno dismounted by the gate. "*Buenas tardes.* This man is my friend. He's been hurt, Deron. Will you help us?"

"How did he get hurt?" Deron looked at Keno, at Garfield, at Keno again. "You came in by the creek. Does this mean there are men after you?"

"Yes. But not for awhile. Now my friend must have proper care. We need your help—a bed first."

"He is—he is shot?"

"Yes."

"How did this happen?" Deron began to tremble. "Why do you bring this trouble to me?"

"When trouble came to you before, I helped. That's why. Now, do you help us?"

"No!" Deron shook his head violently. "I cannot. My sheep... my house... my wife. All that I have is here! You must not ask this of me."

"Look. If the men come, I'll take my friend and leave before harm can come to you and yours. My word on it."

"It will not do," Deron said bitterly. "They will know you were here. They will... God knows what. Kill my sheep, tear down my house. My wife... no!"

"Old man," Keno said softly, "my friend must have a bed. He must have medicine—*quinina*. And you will have to get it, because I cannot be seen."

Deron pointed to the forty-five at Keno's hip. "Tell me with that. That is how all *gringos* ask when they ask a Mexican for anything."

"This *gringo* doesn't. Do you have a shrine in your house, Deron? Then tonight when you pray, ask your God to forgive you for turning away those he sent you in their need."

"Mariana does all the praying in this house," Deron muttered.

"Then maybe she'll remember us to your God. Your saints. Whatever."

Keno turned to his horse, but Deron caught his arm. "No. I have no faith any more, but I know a man's duty. We'll take him inside."

Mariana came flouncing across the yard, her fear momentarily swallowed in indignation. "Florentino! You do not bring *gringos* under this roof!"

"Be quiet, woman. Go in and prepare the bed. When we have brought him in, I will get my horse and go for the *quinina*...."

CHAPTER FIFTEEN

As soon as she came in sight of the Roost's stony base and the trail leading up to her father's stockade mine, Luana saw the lone horse tied in the rock shade and, sitting on a boulder nearby, a stocky, white-haired man puffing on a cigar. He saw her coming and came slowly to his feet. Luana pulled up her mount and almost fell, dropping out of her saddle to run into his arms.

"Pa! Oh Pa. . . ."

He held her tightly, unable to get out words, and then he held her away from him, his eyes hard and bright. His face looked old and haggard, etched with all the lines of his years. Luana knew what he must have gone through in these three days, yet seeing him like this shocked her somehow. Since she was a little girl, she had stood in awed regard of him. There had never been much visible warmth in him, even before her mother had died, and over the years she'd come to think of him as almost impervious.

"They do anything to you, girl? They hurt you any way at all?"

"No, Pa. But—"

"Then let's get up the trail." That quickly, he was brusque again, back in business. "Mean to put Baffin and the others straightway on their trail. You'll tell 'em whatever might be useful. Come on!"

He caught her by the arm, but Luana pulled free and swung firmly to face him. *"Wait,* Pa! Can't you hear me out?"

"Well?"

Luana hesitated. How did you tell a man news like this? By stages, she supposed. There was no really gentle way. "Pa, maybe you'd better sit down again."

"Dammit, girl, out with it!"

"Well—do you know—did you ever meet a man named Tasker?"

"Tasker!" The way that the blood ebbed from his face almost frightened her. "I never mentioned that name to you, not ever. Where'd you hear it?"

"I met him, Pa. I know he—"

His hands shot out to grip her arms with bruising force. "Where'd you see him? Where's he at?"

"Pa, you're hurting...don't!"

He opened his hands slowly, his face colorless. "I got to sit down." He dropped back onto the rock and took off his Stetson and sleeved his forehead, squinting up at her. "Just give it to me slow, girl. You met a Tasker..."

"He's the man was behind this...well, first it was a plan to steal your gold. But that's not important. I *know* that he's the man who kidnapped little Westy nineteen years ago."

"Always suspected it," Westerman whispered. "He was all busted up after...and he wasn't acting right in the head. No way of knowing anything for sure, but I had detectives on his trail. Couldn't turn up hide nor hair. Not a trace all these years...." His eyes snapped to hard focus on her face. "Where'd you see him, girl? No, they wouldn't wait around, would they? But we can pick up the trail from where—"

"No." She placed a hand on his shoulder, as if to keep him from rising. "There's no need. He's dead, Pa."

"Dead?"

"Bone Shefflin killed him. But there's more. There's ... Pa, it's wonderful news! Westy is alive!"

His face went from white to a dirty gray color that really scared her. She had guessed long ago that if there were a hidden unhealed scar somewhere in her father, it centered around the one tragedy to which his kind of man could never become reconciled: the loss of his one male heir.

"The one who called himself Dave Landry, Pa. He's Weston."

The Major patted his face with a bandanna. It was a half-minute before he spoke, and by then a little of his color had returned. "So that's why. That's why he was familiar to both of us. Let's have the whole story, girl."

She talked for ten minutes, watching his face. It was a granite mask again. He had absorbed the fact that Westy was alive, and the several revelations that were connected to it were less palatable.

When she had finished, he frowned at a fixed point somewhere on the horizon. "Sometimes, girl, it's hard for a man to know whether to laugh or cry."

"Somehow," Luana said dryly, "it's hard to picture you doing either."

A smile flicked his mouth. "I laugh on occasion. Now, what're we going to do about this brother of yours?"

She arched her brows. "Surely you're not asking the advice of a mere—"

"Quit it, girl. You been with him the last three days. You seen more than I have of what kind of a man he really is. What's the best way of handling him?"

"Oh. You mean do we hogtie him or do we use

gentler persuasions—but either way he's coming back?"

"He is," Westerman said grimly. "There ain't no question about that. He's my son. Whatever else he is or ain't, he's coming back."

Luana smiled a little. "To start with, I wouldn't take that particular tack with him, or the only way you'll get him back will be in a plumb salivated condition."

"Huh. He's a Westerman, all right."

"That's another thing. He wasn't deliriously overjoyed about being proved a Westerman. And his name isn't Westy—it's Keno."

The Major grimaced. "Anything else?"

"Doesn't that say it all? He's proud, independent —loyal to a friend. I told you he'd have probably returned with me if he'd been certain his friend wouldn't be hung or jailed."

"Goodlemighty, girl! Is that all? Couldn't you *tell* him?"

Luana met his stare calmly. "I told him the truth —I wasn't sure. Suppose that I'd said, Don't worry, Pa will be so overwhelmed, he'll show charity and forgiveness to your comrade in crime—and then you hung Hook Blanding. It would make him your enemy for life."

"But goddammit, I *wouldn't* of hung the bastard! Jailed him either!"

"That's fine," she said tartly, "but I'm not even good at reading minds at short distances, let alone long ones."

Westerman sighed and got to his feet. "All right, all right. Milk's spilt. Let's get up to the Roost and see what we can do about mopping it up."

Luana picked up her reins. He stepped over to give her a hand into the saddle. As she swung up, her traveling cloak fell open. He saw the torn shirtwaist which she had fastened at the shoulder with pins. Where it gaped open, the tender skin was bruised.

"Girl, you been manhandled. You didn't say about that!"

"Oh—Shefflin. He was drunk and—but Westy stopped him. Almost drowned him."

"Shefflin," the Major said softly.

In saddle, the two of them went up the stony trail and picked their way across the crest to the stockade gate. On the platform, Hans Vedder was dozing on guard. The sound of approaching horses brought him awake, and he scrambled hastily to his feet, looking fatly discomfitted.

"Er, oh, heh, it's you, Major. Miss Luana..."

"Open the gate," Westerman said coldly. "Then get Baffin and tell him to come to the corral. Rudirosa and Jubilo too. Look alive!"

Vedder almost fell off the ladder getting to the ground. As soon as he had pulled open the gate and closed it after them, he headed for the bunkhouse. Westerman and Luana rode to the corral, halted their animals by the water trough, and dismounted.

"Pa," Luana said quietly, watching her horse drink. "Before you give them any orders, there's something you should know. I don't want Giles harmed."

Westerman gave her a stare of furious disbelief. "Did I hear you right? You're worried about *him*? A damned confidence man—"

"Why not?" Luana said calmly.

"He's a blackleg scoundrel, that's why not!" A rich flush of temper climbed to Westerman's neck. "He's a kidnapper and a thief! He's trash!"

"And what are we, Pa? What about the Indians you took this valley from before I was born? What about those federal homesteaders you scared off a couple of years ago? What about this mine works set up on property that isn't yours, and what about the people we're robbing?"

"Goddammit, girl! Watch your tongue!"

"Why?" Luana said swiftly. "I mean, if we're going to put a special Westerman interpretation on the laws of God and man, good heavens, can't we at least be consistent?"

"By God, girl, whatever you're saying, say it plain!"

"I told you. I don't want Giles hurt. And I do want him brought back here."

"But *why*, goddammit!"

"I have my reasons."

Westerman took off his Stetson, ran his fingers through his thick gray hair with a growl of fathomless disgust—"Ah-h-h!"—and clapped his hat back on, glaring at her. "I never denied you anything... not that you ever asked for a lot. But *Garfield!*"

Luana smiled. "D'you really think less of him now than you always did? Honor bright now, Pa."

Westerman shook his head dourly. "Come to that, I reckon not. At least he had the gumption to con us—and I set up a pretty fair plan, looks like, to rob us blind. More'n I'd have given him credit for. But he's still a goddam pipsqueak by my lights. You really love that sorry dude?"

Luana held the enigmatic smile. "I told you. I have my reasons."

Baffin and his three companions came out of the bunkhouse and headed this way. Luana bit her lip, watching them.

"Pa, shouldn't you send out more men to search? And don't you think these four are pretty poor choices for the job? Assuming, that is, you don't want anybody hurt."

"Hell, girl, that's why. Baffin and his boys are cool heads. They all been bounty hunters."

"And how many men do you think they've brought back *alive?*"

Westerman smiled grimly. "Why, honey, as many as they been paid to. They're a breed that takes a man's orders when they take his money, and it's their kind of job. I put a big posse of unruly miners and cowhands on Westy's trail, they'd treat it like a holiday, get gunhappy, probably get drinking, and generally botch the whole thing."

Baffin sauntered up and grinned and touched his hat. "Hoddo, Miss Luana. Glad you're back safe. Something, Major?"

"I want you four to track down those fellows— Landry, Catlett, Sheffin, Garfield. I don't care how you take Shefflin. He don't matter, except I'd admire hanging him with my own hands. But the other three—I want 'em brought in *alive.* Understand?"

Baffin glanced at his cohorts, then scratched his cheek. "Tall order, that, Major."

"Think you could fill it for two thousand in greenbacks apiece?"

Baffin pursed his lips in a soundless whistle. "For two thousand apiece, we can sure-hell try."

"Don't try, Baffin, do it. I want Landry, Catlett, and Garfield brought here unharmed—or you don't collect a cent. You can pick up their trail from Eagle Rock. That's rough country, but I been give to understand Rudirosa tracks like an Injun."

"That is no lie," Bartolo Rudirosa said in his sleepy whisper.

"You could ride along, Major," Baffin said.

Westerman shook his head. "This goddam arthritis of mine, I feel every stone in the trail. You can't let no moss grow if you're going to catch 'em, and I'd only slow you."

Baffin tipped up his head and gazed thoughtfully at the sky. "Best bet's to follow 'em to their first camp," he murmured. "Lay up till dark and take 'em asleep. Landry, hm? Catlett—Garfield . . ."

"Alive," repeated Westerman. "And particularly I want young Landry alive." He tapped Baffin's chest with a meaty finger. "If he's hurt any way at all, I'll have your head, mister."

"Oh?" Baffin's brows climbed lazily. "Why's 'at, Major?"

"He's my son. Get your horses."

CHAPTER SIXTEEN

Keno was dozing on a bench in the corner by the fireplace when the noise of a rider approaching Deron's 'dobe jerked him alert. He came to his feet in a catlike motion, sweeping the room with a glance.

The interior of the 'dobe was a single large room, twice as long as it was wide. There was a huge fieldstone fireplace, shelves for food and utensils, and a puncheon table flanked by half-log benches. Pegs driven into the rough brown walls supported strings of peppers, spices, and dried vegetables. In one corner was a bed consisting of a simple log frame with a mattress made of strips of interlaced rawhide. Hook lay on it tossing feverishly, muttering in delirium. Garfield had spread his blankets on the packed-earth floor and was deep in exhausted sleep.

Mariana Deron was kneeling by the fireplace, feeding sticks into the small blaze, sending Keno an occasional venomous glance as she worked. That was why he had fought to keep from going fully asleep. Much as she resented the presence of *gringos*, no telling what she might try during her husband's absence.

The rider must be Deron returning. But as Keno started for the door, he halted—listening. More than one horse coming, or he was a fool. He slid his gun from its holster and ghosted up next to the door, flattening himself against the wall. Mariana looked frightened; he raised a warning finger to his lips.

In a moment Deron wearily pushed open the door and came inside. Somebody was close behind him, a slight-looking youth. Keno snaked out a hand, closed it over the youth's arm as he came across the threshold and yanked him inside. In the same instant Keno drove a heel against the door and slammed it shut. Seizing a fistful of the youth's collar, he wrenched him around and dragged him up on his toes, jamming the gun barrel bruisingly against his throat.

"Boy, if there's any more of you out there, you better tell them—"

He broke off. The face under the slouch hat was that of Tally Jo, the girl from Peggott's. Her eyes flickered with little blue flames.

"And you," she said ominously, "had better take your hand offen me or you'll be the sorriest man alive."

Keno let go and pushed her away, turning an angry stare at Deron. "You crazy? Why bring her here?"

"How do I stop her?" Deron said sullenly. "Peggott was not around, only this one. When I asked for the *quinina,* she wanted to know why I came all the way for it when it's turning dark. What is so wrong, she asked."

"He didn't make answer quick enough," Tally Jo snapped. "So I asked again. Finally got the story."

"*Santa Maria,*" muttered Deron. "She is like a leech, this one. She hangs on till she knows what she wants to."

"Blamed right," Tally Jo said, and set the worn

buckskin bag she was carrying on the table. She took off her hat, then peeled off the old coat she wore. She had on moccasins, a calico shirt, and sacklike trousers that pretty well disguised her burgeoning curves, which took some doing. She began rolling up her sleeves, nodding toward the bed. "How's he now?"

"That's why you came?"

She gave Keno a richly disgusted stare. "Well, why in Tophet you *think*, boy? Listen. I work sixteen hours a day in Peggott's. I put up with stuff from that scum he trades with that I wouldn't put a dog through." She opened the bag and began setting out different articles. "But that Hook man, he never treated me but decent. When he joshed me, it was all in fun, not the mean or grubby sort either."

Keno eyed the things she'd brought. There were Peruvian barks for quinine and other things packed away in small unlabeled bags and boxes. "What's all that?"

"Mountain medicine, boy. My old granny was a herb woman. She willed me all this. Showed me how to make all manner of potions and poultices...."

It was a long night, the longest in Keno's memory. Hook's fever was critically high. Keno had no brief for mumbo-jumbo physic, but he soon found that there was no hocus-pocus about Tally Jo's homespun skills. She was a small, brisk, matter-of-fact dynamo who kept them all hopping for her. To cut the fever, she brewed up a pungent tea from Peruvian barks and red senic, and through the night forced repeated doses down Hook's throat. She cleaned out the wound and made poultices to draw the poison. She cooled Hook's parched skin with wet cloths and kept the others busy fanning him. Keno's attitude passed by stages from skepticism to admiration.

The hours passed. By morning Hook's groanings and twitchings had relaxed; his fever was going down. Keno was relieved, but his mood didn't lose its edge.

Deron and his wife were increasingly jittery, both of them eying all three *gringos* in a way that wished them far gone.

To get away from it, Keno walked outside in the dawn's pink light and paced up and down, working the kinks out of his muscles and the fog out of his brain. He was restless with nerves himself, and a good thing too, for badly as he wanted sleep, he couldn't afford it. The sun was an upbreaking rim of flame in the east, heralding a new day. A day that would bring men on the hunt.

He tried to rap his tired thoughts into a semblance of order. So far he had been taking things a step at a time, not daring to think beyond the moment.

What the hell could he do if and when they came? Stand them off alone? Assessing the help that was available, Deron and Garfield, he tasted hopelessness. He'd promised Deron that they'd evacuate his place if searchers came, but how could Hook be moved now? Hell!

Hearing a footstep behind him, he whirled, hand diving to his gun.

"Boy, you jumpier than a herd o' hoptoads," Tally Jo said. "I only come out to say you best get some sleep."

Keno rasped a hand over his wiry scrub of beard, a gesture of vast weariness. "No sleep."

"You're afeared someone's looking for you, ain't that it? Starting at all kinds of sounds, prowling all the time like a blamed cat."

"Reckon Deron told you."

"Told me what? He don't know nothing but that you come riding in with a bullet-shot friend and that dude in tow. All I was ever sure of, you and that Hook man and the dude and the old scarface fella was up to *something* bad."

Keno shrugged. "Not so bad. We set out to rob a thief."

Her large guileless eyes searched his face. "Thieving is thieving, boy. The who of it don't sugar it none. Wisht you'd tell me about it, though."

"Why?"

Tally Jo scowled, buying a moment's time by ramming in her shirttail, making the shirt strain roundly across her firm and thrusting breasts. She wasn't conscious of the effect—didn't seem to be anyhow. Hard telling what was in a woman's mind. Any woman's.

"Oh, I dunno. Yes, I do. I like you is why. Did right off. I know it ain't seemly, speaking up a-sudden, but there ain't a whole lot of time to build up to it. Leastways there don't seem to be."

Keno didn't know at once what to say, and when he did, it came lamely. "That ain't too smart."

"Smart ain't got a speck to do with it, boy. Anyhow it ain't no concern of yours less'n you want it to be. Maybe I wouldn't a' said it if you didn't look troubled so sore. Talking up on a thing can be easeful. You want me to, I can listen. You want me to go back in, say so."

"No. Don't go in."

For the first time in his life he felt fronted by something he didn't want to face out alone. No physical dilemma had ever cowed him, but this was a different sort. Maybe this strange waif of a girl could help...just by listening.

They walked slowly under the cottonwoods as he talked, telling her everything. He saw the little breaks of compassion, the flashes of wise innocence in her expression as she listened.

At first he felt better for talking. But as he went on, the sense of vacuum he felt crystallized into bitter negations. He was no longer sure what he was, who he was, or what he should try to be.

Tally Jo had no doubts at all.

"You stole from your own pa," she said flatly when he'd finished. "Stealing's wrong enough, but stealing from your pa, why, that's 'most as bad as what Lot's daughters done in the Book!"

"What was that?"

"Well, it was bad, that's all! 'Course you didn't *know* who you was stealing from, but once you did, you was bounden to make it right."

"I returned three shares of the money," Keno said irritably.

"It was you bounden duty to see it was *all* give back. Letting Shefflin and Garfield keep their shares, it's like you stood by and watched your pa being robbed and never lifted a finger."

"I don't figure so," he said stubbornly. "Anyhow I made a bargain with the others and I never went back on my word to a man. That bargain got made first and it had to be kept."

"Listen, boy, talk about firsts! You was your father's son before you was anything, knowing it or not. Once you knowed, you was bounden."

"That's what you say. I ain't no Westerman's son. I'm me, what I always been. That's how I see it."

"Then," Tally Jo said shrewdly, "how come you give back any of that money?"

"Pretty tricky, ain't you?"

"No!" she snapped. "I'm just telling you're straddling fence. You got to jump one way or t'other. What's right to do is the smart thing too. Waiting here all set up to take on your pa's men if they find you, that's plain-out dumb, boy. You'll get yourself shot—then your friend'll get the same. But you take yourself and the rest of that money straightway back to your pa and you'll prob'ly save both your necks."

Keno's jaw hardened; he didn't answer.

"So why *don't* you?" she continued angrily. "I'll tell you why! You're too blamed mean-proud to make sense to yourself. For you, it's a sight easier to just spit in someone's eye. You been doing it all your life, so that's what you do!"

They stopped walking and glared at each other.

Finally he muttered, "I can't do nothing about Shefflin's cut. He taken it with him up in the hills."

It was a victory for Tally Jo. The words had come out of him before he realized it. Before he even had time to feel chagrin, she said swiftly, "All right, but Garfield's inside yonder. You can take his share back, and you can make up with your pa—"

"Listen," he said coldly, furiously, "don't read off to me what I'll do. I'll take back the money—I'll even square away with old Westerman if it'll save Hook. But that's all! Then I ride outen this valley. I ain't a Westerman and I won't live like one."

"All right." Her voice had softened suddenly. "If you say so, you ain't a Westerman. But you ain't what you was, either. A kidnapper and a thief. That's all I'm caring about. Long as you ain't that any more, you can set out to be anything you want."

Her eyes shone up at him. He saw the beginning of a smile curve the corners of her lips. Yes, she'd won. And suddenly he was sure why she cared, but what about him?

He wasn't sure. Not yet.

"You figure that you have straightened me out and now you have got a claim on me?"

"Not less'n you say so. But you look at me hard."

"I'm looking."

"You reckon you could learn to have a feeling for me?"

He had to laugh. "Tally Jo, that'd be no trick at all."

"Well," she said solemnly, "it all starts with that, boy. The rest will come."

He grinned, not knowing what to make of this

waif and her bright talent for heading off his thoughts. She had candor and honesty and not a mote of hesitation about speaking her mind. He had the rather startled thought that if a man did want to start a new life, he could do a sight worse than try it in tandem with Tally Jo. Her young life was being wasted at Peggott's...and that was something else. Maybe they could help each other.

It all starts with that. The rest will come.

He raised his hands to her firm waist, then slid them downward to the flaring hips whose femininity wasn't quite concealed even by the rough trousers. Tally Jo's eyes widened; her lips parted. She made a little noise in her throat and came suddenly into him, her mouth seeking his, the press of her body and arms quick and passionate. He felt the thrusting tautness of her young breasts against his chest, tasted the sweet moving wetness of her mouth under his lips. When they stepped apart, her eyes were shining.

"Oh, whee-oo, oh man, we won't have no trouble, but you got to take off that scratchy beard."

He was shaken. "We better go back in."

They walked back to the 'dobe. Deron was splitting wood in the yard, wielding the ax with the stiff, jerky violence of a worried man. He ceased chopping and sleeved a trickle of sweat from his balding dome.

"*Señor,* if men come—" he began.

"Quit fretting," Keno told him. "We're going to set it right."

An aroma of fresh coffee hit their faces as they entered the house. Hook was resting comfortably, and Garfield, who had been dead to the world since rolling into his blankets last night, was just groaning himself to a sitting position on the floor. His face, with its sooty growth of beard, looked more jowly and raffish than ever.

He stared groggily at Tally Jo. "You," he said stupidly.

"How's your hand feel?" she asked expressionlessly.

Keno didn't mince words. "You're out money, Garfield. I'm taking that ten thousand back to Westerman.

Garfield's face collapsed like melting suet. He was at a loss for words, and it was a rare moment. "You can't do that," he said finally, feebly.

"You might be surprised."

"But *why?*" Garfield bleated.

"Not for any reason you'd understand. You better come along too."

"M-m-me?" Garfield stuttered. "Oh no no no, you can't expect me to...!"

"Up to you," Keno said indifferently. "But I'm staying in the valley a spell. If you go, you go alone, and you ain't got much belly for the idea. You stay here, you'll be found sure, maybe strung up on the spot."

"Yes," Garfield said miserably.

"Other hand, if you come with me to see Westerman, I'll give it out you had a change of heart and want to return your piece of the money. It's the best chance all around, Garfield."

"Yes," Garfield said miserably. "It sounds just fine."

CHAPTER SEVENTEEN

"Well, there he is, *amigo*," Rudirosa murmured to Baffin. "How do we take him?"

"Could pot him from here easy as not," growled Jubilo. "Wouldn't be an almighty long shot for that big ole Sharps o' yourn, Roddy."

"Not while there's a chance he can tell us where the others went," Baffin said, chewing on his cold cigar and not taking his eyes off the small camp.

"Then what we waiting on?" grumbled Hans Vedder, shifting his solid-fat bulk uncomfortably against the rocks.

The four men sprawled at the flinty rim of a ridge overlooking a little brush-grown amphitheater set in the boulder-studded swale below. The sky had barely grayed into pre-dawn, bringing detail out of the pale murk that still cloaked the surrounding hills.

Yesterday, arriving at Eagle Rock to pick up the trail of Luana Westerman's kidnappers, they had found the track split apart. One man had headed south, and Bartolo Rudirosa had quickly identified the broken gait of his horse: Bone Shefflin's. The other three had gone southwest, and Baffin had put Rudirosa on that trail. But it had soon petered out on a cunningly chosen route of rock and large rubble. Even Rudirosa's skills weren't equal to ferreting out a sign on such terrain.

Cursing their luck, the four had returned to Eagle Rock, where Rudirosa began to laboriously spell out the sign left by the lone horseman, Shefflin.

It had been hard going at first. The wolfer had been careful about his trail till he had reached the first hills to the south. Then he had gotten cocky: this was his country. He had followed his favorite trails, some of which were well defined enough to make tracking easy. Rudirosa had lost the spoor a few times in the upland maze of boulder fields and old trails, but always he'd found it again.

At sunset they had made a cold dry camp and had shivered out the night in the chilly heights. They had wolfed cold food and had caught a few snatches of sleep, huddling together for warmth, not daring a fire, not even the comfort of a cigarette. They might have been miles away from Shefflin or only yards away.

As it happened, they had sat out the long night not a hundred yards from his own fireless camp. As the sky had begun to lighten, a horse had neighed faintly from beyond a ridge. One of their animals had answered, but apparently it hadn't wakened Shefflin. By the time the four men had scrambled to the summit of the ridge and seen the camp below, Shefflin was still a silent shape in his blankets.

"That wolfer's a tricky 'un," Jubilo muttered. "Could be just a pile o' blankets planted down there and he's off in the rocks som'eres."

"That's your answer," said Vedder.

A few seconds later the blankets stirred; Shefflin rumbled in his sleep, then settled down again.

Baffin grinned. "And there's *my* answer," he whispered. "All right, Rudy, go on down and get the drop. Wouldn't trust nobody else to do it on the quiet."

"I don't see his rifle," Rudirosa murmured, "but he has the *pistola* too, maybe under the blankets. And do not forget that knife. If he goes for any of them?"

"You usually shoot for the heart, don't you, Rudy?"

"That is a foolish question, *amigo mio.*"

"And hit it too," Baffin said. "So you can wing a man just as easy. We need him alive."

"*Sí.*"

Rudirosa eased to his feet and passed like a gaunt cat over the crown of the ridge and down its flank, slithering between the giant boulders in utter silence. The *pistolero* must be well into his fifties, Baffin thought, but he moved with all the lean grace and economy of a twenty-year-old.

Shefflin's nag pricked up his ears as he watched the Mexican's descent, but he made no noise. Rudirosa reached the base of the ridge and edged into the brushy amphitheater. He skirted the pack of Shefflin's gear and halted a foot from the prone man, then slipped out his gun and bent down and cocked it a few inches from Shefflin's ear, all in one fluid motion.

The wolfer groaned and snored on. Rudirosa nudged him with a foot. Shefflin came suddenly to his senses, his eyes whipping up and around. He was on his side, turned away from the Mexican, and now he moved like lightning, his body spinning face-up even as his hand—holding a pistol—flung the blanket aside in coming around.

Rudirosa's boot lashed out. Shefflin howled as the toe caught him in the wrist and sent the gun flying.

"You move around too much." Rudirosa grinned his death's-head grin. "Up—up. On your feet, stinking one."

Shefflin crawled out of his tangled blankets, rub-

bing his wrist, as Baffin and Vedder and Jubilo
came scrambling down off the ridge.

"Jube, get that knife. Hans, look through his
pack." Baffin stood with his hands lightly on his
hips, scanning the camp. He saw Shefflin lick
his lips and send a quick, nervous glance at some
rocks to his right. Baffin gave the rocks a brief look-
over and saw the steel of a rifle barrel wink dully
in the gray light. Shefflin had left the weapon leaning between two rocks, half-concealed by brush.

Jubilo ambled over and bent and yanked the
wolfer's knife from its boot sheath. He tested its
edge with the ball of his thumb, cut himself, swore,
and flung the knife far away.

Shefflin's yellow-tinged eyes blinked sullenly.
"You musta found them others. They put you onto
me."

"Nope," Baffin grinned. "You was clumsy was all,
Bone."

Vedder kicked the loose pack apart and shoved
the various articles around him with an indifferent
foot. "No gun," he announced.

"It's his cut of the fifty thousand we're looking
for," Baffin snapped. "Where is it, Bone?"

"I dig it out, you let me go?"

"If you do not dig it out, spick hater," Rudirosa
purred, "I will blow one of your feet off. Then the
other. Then your manhood. Maybe some stinking
gringa will weep for that."

Shefflin blinked, yellow-eyed and fearful. He
looked at Baffin. "I give you the money, you don't
let him do nothing?"

"You got my word."

"Don't shoot, now. I got to get in my shirt."

"Go ahead."

Shefflin carefully raised the buckskin shirt. A
money belt was cinched around his gaunt white
belly. He undid it and held it out.

"Drop it," Baffin said.

Shefflin let the belt slip from his fingers. Once more his glance slid warily toward the rifle propped in the rocks.

Baffin said amusedly, "Pay attention now, Bone. We want to hear about Landry and the other two."

"Uh, yeh, well, I ain't nowise sure. Listen, why'n't you tell that greaser to put away his gun?"

"Told you, he ain't going to hurt you none. My word. What you mean, you ain't sure? You see which way they went?"

"Hell, no, I taken off for the hills afore they left Eagle Rock. But Landry now—real name's Keno or maybe Westy—"

"We know that."

"Well, that Hook got a bullet in him and was pluperfect close to death, so Landry said he 'uz going to take 'em to Deron's. That's when I decided to split off. Garfield, reckon he went with 'em, but don't know for sure."

"Who the hell is Deron? Where's his place?"

Shefflin gave some rough directions. "But I opine they ain't there. That yallerbelly greaser ain't gonna chance his own brown hide to save nobody."

"Well, we'll go have a look just in case," Baffin said pleasantly, and nodded toward the rifle. "Go get it, Bone."

Shefflin's jaw gaped. "You want that greaser to dust me!"

"Nothing of the sort. Just admire to have a look at that rifle. Fetch it over, Bone."

Shefflin stared at him a long moment, then turned and moved toward the rifle at his shambling gait. As he bent to pick it up, Baffin saw his shoulders tense. Rudirosa was smiling, his cocked pistol balanced lightly in his hand. Baffin knew that as soon as Shefflin had his hands on the gun, he would make the desperate play of any man with nothing to lose. And in that instant Rudirosa would gun him down.

Shefflin bent, picked up the rifle and started to straighten about. Baffin pulled his forty-five, palmed it up, and fired. Shefflin was knocked spinning like a rag dervish. Baffin coldly cocked the pistol and shot again, driving the wolfer's body back into the rocks.

Rudirosa spoke, his tone soft and wicked. "You knew that I wanted the stinking one, *amigo*. You knew it!"

"Sure," Baffin said idly as he replaced the two spent loads. "But I give him my word, didn't I? Let's see that poke, Hans."

Vedder handed him the money belt. Baffin spread it out on a rock and emptied the pockets one by one. He counted out ten thousand one hundred and fifty dollars. The one hundred and fifty, also in crisp new bills, would be the bounty money that Westerman had paid the wolfer. There was nothing else of value.

Baffin mentally divided by four and began counting the large denomination bills into four separate stacks.

"What you doing, Roddy?" asked Jubilo.

Baffin didn't bother to glance up. "What's it look like?"

Jubilo chuckled, a little uneasily. "Looks like the Major hain't gonna get back his ten thousand."

"Wouldn't surprise me none if you're right," Baffin murmured. "Seeing's he didn't bid high enough. Not with five thousand apiece on the table." He finished his count and stood up, pocketing one stack of money. "Pick up your shares and let's get riding."

Jubilo furrowed his brow. "Five thousand apiece? That don't cipher out to...oh."

"Yes," Baffin said dryly. "According to what Miss Luana told, there oughta be another ten thousand waiting at this Deron's."

"When we have it," Rudirosa said thinly, "we will have to ride from here fast. And very far."

"Well, Mexico's your stamping ground, ain't it?" Baffin turned and tramped up the slope. "Come on. We're wasting time...."

Though they didn't spare their horses, the sun was high in the morning blue when they came in sight of the straggling emerald line of shrubbery that marked the creek's twisting course across the summer-blasted valley floor. They followed it upstream. By midmorning they came to the squat adobe shack set in the cottonwood park.

They halted their animals behind a screen of trees some hundred yards from the 'dobe. A thread of smoke trickled from the chimney, but there was no way of telling how many people were inside. No horses in sight either.

"We'll work in close," Baffin said, "but stay behind the trees as you go. There's no windows on this side, but go careful."

They dismounted and tied their animals, then crept along single file through the veiling shade and leaves. They reached the 'dobe's southwest corner and flattened along the wall on the side away from the paddock.

Listening, Baffin could hear small movements inside, no other sounds. He nodded at his companions and then, gun in hand, slipped around the corner and edged up to the doorway, the others close behind. The door was propped open. Baffin cocked his pistol as he stepped swiftly across the threshold.

A plump, olive-skinned girl was seated in a rocking chair with some mending, and at the table a slight, balding Mexican was drinking coffee. They must have been riding a tight edge, for both jumped like a pair of shot rabbits.

"Hold still," Baffin said.

He took in the room with a glance. It was empty except for the Mexican couple and the blanket-covered form of Hook Blanding on the bed. Hook was flushed with fever, twitching in his sleep. Baffin walked to the bed and studied him a moment, then glanced at Deron.

"Where's the others?"

Deron gave him a sullen dark-eyed stare and didn't answer. Baffin motioned brusquely and said, "Ask him, Rudy."

Rudirosa spoke in rapid Spanish. Deron replied with a word or two and shook his head.

"He says he doesn't know."

"Tell him he's being a goddam fool. What's he owe any *gringo?*"

Rudirosa smiled, a little thinly. "A good question, *amigo.*" He spoke to Deron again. Another short sullen reply and headshake.

"Landry and Garfield, they probably miles from here by now," Vedder observed.

"Like hell," Baffin said flatly. "That Landry wouldn't run out on a partner. Not unless I read him way wrong."

He paused. The voiced thought had given rise to a more uncomfortable one. Landry might have taken the precaution of concealing himself outside somewhere. He might be covering the shack right now....

"Rudy, get outside and look for sign. And watch yourself."

Rudirosa glided out the door. Baffin walked to the fireplace. He gazed at the crumbling bed of coals, then looked at Deron. He knew from the Mexican's perceptible reactions to their talk that he understood English.

"Listen to me, old man. You're going to tell us about them other two. And the money. It's up to you."

Deron said nothing.

"Hans, suppose you give that woman's arm a twist."

Vedder was already eying the plump girl with a brutal, slack-lipped lust that was transparent. He

started toward her. She came uncertainly to her
feet, then tried to duck past him. Vedder's clublike
hand caught a handful of her blouse; it ripped as he
yanked her off balance. His other hand closed on a
smooth brown arm and wrenched it up a painful
angle behind her back.

"Tell it, old man," Baffin said.

Deron stood up, leaning his hands on the table,
his eyes like live coals. Vedder, his sweaty face close
to the girl's, twisted hard. A short scream escaped
her.

Deron came around the table, lunging for the pile
of cordwood stacked by the hearth. He scooped up a
chunk and raised it above his head and ran at Vedder, whose back was to him. Deron brought the
chunk down in a blind arc, slamming the thickset
man across the shoulders.

Vedder howled and let go of the girl. He came
lumbering around, his face scarlet. "You spick bastard—"

"Let it go, Hans," Baffin said amusedly. "Grab
aholt of the Mex, both of you. There's a quicker
way."

Vedder and Jubilo both moved in on Deron, who
dropped the billet and backed off from them till his
shoulders touched the wall. They seized his arms.
Baffin sauntered over to the girl, who cowered away
from him. He seized a thick handful of her black
hair and dragged her to the hearth and forced her
down on her knees.

"Watch this now, Mex...."

With his free hand he locked both the girl's
wrists behind her back, then pushed her face down
till it was inches from the cherried bank of coals.
She screamed and screamed again.

"Let her go, *amigo*."

It was Rudirosa's whisper-soft voice. He stood in
the doorway. He hadn't drawn his gun, nor did he

have to. Vedder and Jubilo were occupied with
Deron; Baffin was bent over holding the girl. With
his speed, Rudirosa could take all of them before
they could get into action.

Baffin said in a tone of quiet fury, "Don't be a
goddam fool, Rudy!"

"Blood is thicker than gold, *amigo*. If you hurt a
Mexican woman in front of Rudirosa, why then
you're the fool."

He meant it, Baffin saw. He released the girl and
stood back. Rudirosa moved smoothly into the room
and over to the bed. He looked speculatively down
at Hook Blanding.

"*Amigos,* there were three here who have gone.
Landry and Garfield and a woman."

Baffin, his eyes warm and dangerous, stared at
him. "What woman?"

"I don't know. I found where their horses had
been hidden. In some trees down by the creek. This
one's horse is still there. I could follow them, but
this would take time."

"Too damned much time! What do you—"

Rudirosa whipped the blanket off Hook's prone
form. He saw the bandaged leg and gently nodded.
"So." He pulled his knife and deliberately cut the
bandages away, exposing the swollen, discolored
flesh. It seemed to be smeared with a poultice of
some kind.

Rudirosa lightly flicked the vicinity of the wound
with his knifepoint. Hook jerked and gave an explosive grunt. Rudirosa glanced at Deron. Smiling
faintly, he said something in Spanish. Then he increased the knife's pressure on the tortured flesh.
Hook groaned, his head thrashing back and forth.

"No," Deron said.

"You can stop it, *viejo,*" Rudirosa said, his words
so clear and slow that Baffin could follow the Spanish with no difficulty. "Tell us where they went."

He pressed down on the knife. Blood welled up around the tip. Hook let out a bull bellow and reared half upright, then fell back again.

"Don't." Deron's face was gray. He looked tired and sick and beaten, his voice almost inaudible above his wife's low sobbing. "I will tell."

CHAPTER EIGHTEEN

By the time Keno called a noon halt, they had covered about two-thirds of the distance to Westerman's Roost. He was in no hurry for the confrontation with the grim-eyed man he now knew was his father. He tried to think about how it would go and what he should say, and no answers came.

He and Tally Jo and Garfield sat in a baking boulder field and ate a meager lunch. The girl had little to say; she was content with the new turn her life had taken, armed with a conviction that all would turn out well. Garfield, however, worried aloud about anything and everything connected with the possible consequences of his throwing himself on the Major's mercy.

Keno ignored him, puzzling out his own feelings. Just looking at Tally Jo made him feel better. Whatever happened, she would be there. And he thought of later. The three of them, he and Tally Jo and Hook, could go down to Mexico and start over the right way....

"Let's get going," he said.

He had gotten to his feet and half-turned toward his horse when he saw a yellow banner of dust climbing into the sky across the flats. At least one horseman was coming fast, but he was still too far away for Keno to tell anything.

Garfield followed his gaze. "Who's that?"

Keno didn't take his eyes off the dust. "Want to go ask him?"

"No," Garfield said nervously. "I just think we'd better get out of here."

"And I think we better wait. He's coming from the same direction as us."

His first thought was that Hook, whom they'd left resting though still feverish, might have taken a sudden turn for the worse and that Deron had come after him. For the moment he didn't think beyond that. They had to wait.

The sun-hued dance of saffron clouds began to lessen, breaking into the dark shapes of four riders. They were much closer now, and they were slowing a little—as if they had seen the trio.

"Look at that!" Garfield said. "Four of them. We'd better make a run—"

"If they're after us and we run and they catch up to us in the open, we're in real trouble."

As he spoke, Keno studied the rise of land to their left. It was a jumble of abutting boulders over-run by rioting brush. "Get into that," he told Garfield and Tally Jo. "It's cover if need be, and we can palaver from there."

They walked their horses to the rise, pulling them along through the rock cover, and filtered into the giant boulders on the lower rise. Keno cramped himself between a couple of slabs and raised himself enough to get a view of the approaching riders. When they had reined to a dusty halt a little way off, he recognized Roddy Baffin and his cohorts.

"That's far enough, Baffin! What're you after?"

"Not a thing, bucko," Baffin yelled. "Satisfaction, maybe. We aim to return you to your daddy. He sent us for that."

"We're heading for the Roost now. We don't need no escort."

"Listen, bucko. We found your partner at Deron's. He told us where you was going. Thing is, the Major made us an offer of two thousand apiece, we bring you back without a hair o' your head singed. You bring yourself in, how do we collect? Come on, now. All we want is to ride in with you-all. Man, it ain't worth a fight."

"Hook told you, eh?"

"That's what I said, bucko."

"That's how I heard you, and you're a damned liar. You could roast Hook and he wouldn't of told you where I was. Deron, likely. But not Hook."

Baffin pulled his prancing horse around on a hard rein. "Bucko, you're coming out, like I said. It don't matter how. You got a woman with you. We know that. You want her getting hurt?"

Keno was silent a moment. Then: "Just what d'you want, Baffin?"

"Ten thousand dollars. Toss it out here. Then we ride away."

Tally Jo was laid up behind a rock a few yards from Keno. She left cover and ran to his side, ducking low, and dropped on her knees, seizing his arm. "Don't you dast give 'em that money! It ain't yours to give!"

"That ain't the point," Keno said bleakly.

"It is! If I wasn't here, you'd give 'em the holy what-for before you'd let 'em ride off with it! Listen. You give 'em the money and you'll never see me again!"

"Keep your head down," Keno said wearily. He raised his voice again. "No good, Baffin. Back off out of here or we start shooting. And there's three of us."

"Yeah," Baffin laughed. "Some help you got, bucko."

He wheeled his mount and rode off a short distance, then pulled to a halt by the boulder field. Piling swiftly out of his saddle, he yanked his rifle from its scabbard and dived for cover. The others followed suit. Keno sent a snap shot at Vedder's fat legs and missed.

Baffin didn't waste time or ammunition laying down a fire at the rocky breastworks where they were sheltered. In a moment Keno saw the lithe form of Bartolo Rudirosa sprint briefly into view, moving away from them. Then the tangle of rock swallowed him. A moment later Jubilo's lank shape followed, then Vedder's chunky one.

"What are they doing?" Garfield whispered.

Keno twisted a glance toward the rocky mass of the rise towering at their backs. "Working around to get above us. Probably at different places. Take us in a crossfire."

"Good God," Garfield said faintly. "Can't you give them the money?"

Keno left his boulder, crawled over to where Garfield was sprawled, and seized him by the shoulder. "Buck up, damn you! I got to leave you and get up above here before they do. She ain't got no rifle. You have. You're going to have to hold 'em off from here."

Garfield's face screwed up like a pale prune. "I-I-I think I'm going to be sick."

"Huh-uh. You ain't. And I'll tell you why. If you fold and they get close enough for anything to happen to her—and both you and me come out alive, you won't stay alive five minutes after."

"I'll take his blamed rifle," Tally Jo said disgustedly.

"You ever fired one?"

She hesitated. "Some."

"No you ain't. Keep down and keep still."

Holding his body crouched, Keno moved to the edge of the sheltering rocks and peered at the curving slope beyond.

Baffin alone had stayed where he was, waiting to pot them if they left the rocks. If he could get around that curve, though, he would be cut off from Baffin's fire....

He lunged suddenly to his feet and, bent almost double, made a run for it. Baffin began firing as fast as he could level his rifle. Keno heard the slugs whine off rocks left and right of him.

He had nearly reached shelter when he felt a numbing blow that tore the rifle from his hand. A few more straining feet and he achieved a rock and dropped behind it. He could see his rifle lying yards away, the stock splintered. The bullet had struck it only inches from his grip on the mechanism. His left hand was so numb he could hardly move it.

Anyway he wasn't left-handed. And a rifle wasn't really his weapon.

He worked his fingers till feeling returned to the hand, and with it a wincing soreness. Then he took the time to remove his boots. Afterward he began a noiseless ascent of the rise, moving warily but swiftly in his sock feet across sun-scorched rocks that were like red-hot plates. The summit of the rise was literally composed of massive boulders that looked as if they had been flung there in jumbled confusion by a titanic hand.

There was a burst of rifle fire from down below: apparently Baffin and Garfield exchanging a few shots. Then silence again.

A scrape of boot on rock was startlingly close, alerting him. Keno shrank down against the ground, listening, the good, familiar weight of his Colt slightly sweaty against his hand. He saw nothing, heard nothing more. Easing cautiously to his feet again, he edged forward till he topped a rimrock that dropped suddenly off to the slope.

Not thirty feet below him was Hans Vedder, working into position on a ledge above Garfield and

Tally Jo. And Garfield's tweed-clad back was clear in Vedder's sights as he raised his rifle to his shoulder.

"Hans! Behind you!"

Baffin had yelled the words, leaping to his feet and cupping both hands to his mouth. Garfield promptly fired, causing him to drop down again.

"Drop it, Vedder!"

The chunky gunman ignored the order. He came wheeling about wildly, swinging up his rifle. Keno broke his shoulder with a bullet, knocking him off his feet and sending his rifle clattering off the ledge.

Keno faded swiftly back from the rimrock. Vedder was out of the fight, but his painful groans could lure the other two. Keno wedged his back between a couple of rocks and sank onto his haunches, waiting. He heard small rattles of pebbly sound. A man was climbing this way through the forest of rock.

Suddenly he halted, still out of sight. Evidently he feared a trap. He would come no farther, Keno guessed, until the third man had joined him.

Keno had fixed the man's location from his last movement. *Why wait?* He rose to his feet and slipped silently along through the rocks. Skirting a vast cluster of boulders, he saw a blocky crumbling abutment just beyond it. Keno came around between the rock cluster and the abutment where they crowded nearly together. Flattening his back almost against the abutment flank, he moved like a cat toward where it angled sharply out of sight.

He came abruptly around the angle, pivoting into the clear. Jubilo was leaning against the abutment off-guard, and a look of total surprise seized his gaunt face. His pistol was out and he was starting to bring it up when Keno fired. The slug's impact slammed Jubilo against the rock. He slid down until he was sitting, bowed over with pain, hugging the far left side of his chest.

"You bagged old Jube for fair, boy...hope they get you."

Keno ignored him. He knew that Jubilo wasn't seriously wounded. He paused only long enough to scoop up the man's fallen pistol and ram it in his belt; then he was restlessly questing the shimmering terrain with his eyes. Where was Rudirosa?

"Over here, Rudy," Jubilo bawled.

Keno moved swiftly away, swinging noiselessly through the rocks till he was out of Jubilo's view. Then he halted, crouching again. A lone buzzard made a wheeling dot against the white-blue sky. No sound. No movement at all. He blinked away sweat and moved on....

He had nearly reached the north side of the hill when suddenly below he caught a dark flicker of motion. He fired, at the same time plunging down over the rim in a reckless run. Rudirosa fired back, dusting his boots with rock chips.

Just ahead of him, Keno saw a shallow defile spring into view. Not breaking pace, he dropped into it and kept moving downslope, now hidden by its tall banks from Rudirosa's line of fire. He was nearly to the bottom, only yards from the Mexican's position, when he stopped. Digging in his toes, he climbed the bank till his eyes topped the rim.

There was no sign of Rudirosa where he had last seen him, only the sullen dance of heat off bare stone. Keno listened. Silence had dropped like a dead hand on the hot scape.

Suddenly he heard a rough whisper of cloth over rock. His mouth tightened. Rudirosa had taken off his boots too. He watched, but the steps paused. Keno marked the place with his eyes. Then, softly sliding Jubilo's pistol from his belt, he lobbed it overhead away to his left. It crashed among the rocks.

Rudirosa leaped out from his shelter, arcing his gun around to cover the sound. Too late he saw Keno surging up across the cutbank and knew he'd been tricked. His gun swung back like lightning. The two men fired at the same time.

Rudirosa's light frame was jarred back on its heels, but he didn't go down. He staggered toward Keno, pumping bullets as he came. Keno felt the nip of a slug at his side. He pulled the sights to the *pistolero*'s chest and shot again, carefully. This time Rudirosa went down. He rolled on his side and strained up one elbow, trying to bring his pistol to bear. Then his brown fist relaxed and thudded on the ground, and he slumped over on his face.

Keno felt his legs quivering, giving way, and he let himself drop to his knees. His side was numb at first, then a tearing pain hit. He held himself that way, a hand clamped on his bleeding ribs, till the first agonized spasm had ebbed. He tore open his shirt and saw that the deep bloody scrape wasn't serious, but the bullet, catching a short rib at an angle, must have fractured it.

"That's nice, bucko. Hold still now."

He raised his head. Baffin had stepped into view, standing about forty feet away. He had left his position to maneuver around this way.

Keno had laid down his pistol to examine his wound, and he was on his knees. Helpless, he watched Baffin bring the rifle to his shoulder, his teeth streaking white where his jaw nestled the stock.

The shot came, but not from Baffin's rifle. He was plunging on his face across the round slab where he stood. He managed to heave over on his back and with a great effort raised his head as if to make out who had shot him. Then his head dropped back.

Garfield came creeping into sight, rifle held at the ready, darting wary glances around him. Then he saw how his shot had dropped Baffin, in an arch-backed sprawl across the slab, his head hanging off it.

"Oh," Garfield said, looking greenish. He sat weakly down on the earth, making noises like a sick rooster. Then Tally Jo was running over the rocks toward Keno, and he paid no more attention to Garfield.

CHAPTER NINETEEN

It was late afternoon when they approached the stockade and hailed the guard, who stood up on his platform and simply stared. The five of them were quite a sight, Keno supposed. Both Vedder and Jubilo, their torsos misshapen with crude bandaging, were slumped in their saddles, barely hanging on. Keno was holding himself erect only by a vast effort of will, keeping his arm tightly pressed over the fractured rib and fancying he could feel it crack at every step his horse took.

"Westerman might like to see us," Keno said.

The guard was one of the regular miners, from his clothes and workboots. He blinked. "Yeah. I expect he might."

He descended to the ground and opened the gate. When they had ridden in and turned their horses into the corral, Keno told the guard to help Vedder and Jubilo to the bunkhouse and see that a watch was put on them. Afterward Keno headed for the Major's cabin, Tally Jo walking close at his side, not offering the help he wouldn't ask for but keeping a watchful eye on him just in case. Garfield, having no relish at all for this, lagged behind them.

Keno's knock brought Hessie to the door. Her

long dark face broke in a smile. "Mister Weston!
Come in, sir."

He snapped, "It's Keno," as he followed Tally Jo
inside.

The Major and Luana had been talking quietly
when the door opened, but both were already on
their feet and coming forward.

Keno halted, his boots solidly braced against the
deep carpet, one hand still holding his side. With
the other he held out a thick wad of greenbacks.
The stony and forbidding look he wore made both
Westermans stop halfway across the room.

"Baffin's dead," he said tonelessly. "So's Rudirosa.
They was after the money. Vedder and Jubilo ain't
much hurt. We brought 'em back and you can do
what you want with 'em."

Mechanically the Major took the thick packet. He
gave it the briefest of glances. "The rest of the
money?"

"It's all there. Twenty thousand dollars. Garfield's and Shefflin's shares. Shefflin split off from
us, and Baffin and the others must of found him
because we found ten thousand split among the four
of 'em."

The Major nodded, a little dazedly. "I see. You
brought it all back, West—er, ah, *Keno* is it?"

"That's right. Only Garfield here, he's fetching
back his own share." It was a lie, but he had promised, in order to chop off Garfield's ceaseless worried
yammering, to fabricate a little on the con man's
behalf. Anyway he owed him that much. "Saved my
life too. Got Baffin as he was about to gun me
down."

"*He* did?" The Major jabbed an incredulous finger
at his daughter's erstwhile fiancé. "That goddam
pipsqueak?"

"Pa," Luana murmured in reproval. "Is that any
way to talk about the hero of the day?" She glided
forward and took Garfield's arm, guiding him to the

divan. "For heaven's sake, Giles, sit down before you fall down."

The Major shook himself like a man coming out of a trance. He frowned at the brown stains on Keno's shirt under his hand. "You get hit, boy?"

"A scratch." Keno wanted nothing so much as to sink into one of the deep chairs, but he held himself straight as a gun barrel, his legs stiffly braced. "I came to bring the money back and make my peace with you. That's all. You got no objection, we'll be leaving now."

"We?" Westerman seemed to notice the girl for the first time. His frown deepened. "Who are you, young woman?"

"Tally Jo Richland." Tally Jo's tone was rather subdued. She was taking in the room's fine furnishings, detail by detail, and looking a bit overawed.

"And my s—the boy's going away with you?"

"I thought so till this minute," Tally Jo said slowly. Her gaze had come to rest on Luana's wine-colored dress. "I never seen such a frock. All shiny and crackly-rich like that. What d'you call it?"

"Taffeta," Luana said. She rose and came over to the girl and took her hands. "Tally Jo . . . won't you stay with us? Won't you make him stay?"

Tally Jo shook her head. "He'll stay, I reckon. I'll ask him to. But not me."

Keno swung a narrow glance at her. "What kind of foolish palaver you onto now?"

"This here lady is your sister. And all this here" —she sent a quick circling look around the room—"it's yours. And a right smart more where this come from, I reckon."

"Tally Jo, that's no kind of sense."

"It's sense!" She jerked her hands from Luana's. Her voice held even, but she was fighting tears. "Look at her hands. All tiny small and soft as butter. Look at mine—half again as big, all red 'n' rough! These is your people! Your kind!"

She started to turn blindly toward the door, but Keno grabbed her by the arms. "You ain't getting away that easy. You sit down." He marched her to a chair and seated her in it.

Garfield got to his feet with a nervous chuckle. "Well, *I'll* be leaving, if no one objects."

"You do that, boy," Westerman said. "No charges pressed, nothing said. Just get the hell out of here."

"Just a moment, Pa," Luana said coldly. "I wanted him brought here, or have you forgotten?"

"No," growled the Major. "Wish you would, though."

Garfield stared at her, slack-jawed. "You," he said, "you wanted me..." A kind of dread entered his face. "Why, why, why would you want..."

"That's a good question," she said reflectively. "Why? You have a certain vacuous charm. And a certain species of weasel wit. And almost no redeeming qualities whatsoever."

"Huh huh," Garfield brayed desperately, "very true!" He began to edge toward the door. "So you won't object if—"

"I certainly will." Luana walked over to him and tucked her hand in his arm. "You asked me to marry you, remember? Do you want to be sued for breach of promise. Although"—her laughter tinkled like tiny bells—"that would be the very least of your worries."

"You-you-you wouldn't threaten me with—oh no, Luana!"

"Oh yes, Giles."

The tigress had emerged from this tender, quiet girl like a butterfly from a chrysalis—and the tigress was flexing its bright, sharp claws for all to see as it purred on ever so softly.

"Your nefarious days and ways are at an end, my friend. You will become a willing, respectable, and wholly satisfactory husband, or we'll press enough charges to—well, let's not be unpleasant. And for the same reason, you'll *never* try to run off, will you, Giles?"

Garfield looked at her with a slow mounting fear in his eyes. He had good reason for it, Keno thought. His newfound sister had all her father's steel—and that kind of woman needed complete control over whatever hapless male she chose for a mate. She could love only the man she could dominate—and in this erring groom-to-be, holding the perfect club over his head, she had found an ideal she could look down to.

Not so strange either, Keno reflected. The world was full of women like Luana. She was simply more honest than the others. She knew exactly what she wanted and went after it with all claws unsheathed.

"Let's go for a walk, darling, and discuss every little thing, shall we?"

She guided Garfield toward the door. The con man was numb-faced, silent for once. He wore the stricken look of a deer backed into a cage and seeing the trapgate crash down.

Luana paused at the doorway and said to Keno, "Why don't you think about it?" She smiled and nodded at Tally Jo. "She *can* fit, you know. She's lovely. And that figure! Intelligent—that's obvious. A little training in speech, etiquette, deportment— and just picture her in a gown, with her hair fixed.... Come along, Giles."

"My name is Bill Lutz," Garfield muttered.

"Lutz? Ugh! It sounds like a butcher's name. From now on, darling, you are, to all intent and purpose, Giles Garfield."

The door closed behind them. Keno looked stonily at Major Lewis B. Westerman.

"I want to ask just one thing. My partner's hurt. Blanding—you knew him as Catlett. Left him with a Mexican and his wife. Do what you want with me. Just leave him and them Mexicans alone."

The Major gestured impatiently. "I already promised Luana as much. And you know all that I want of you."

"Spell it out."

"Well, Luana...reckon I underestimated her all this time. She's turned out like the son I never got to raise. But a man wants a real son. One who'll walk in his steps. He wants that more'n anything."

He paused. Keno said nothing.

"You don't make it easy for a man, boy. I can't order you. I can only ask. Stay on. Stay, and it'll all be yours."

"One day. Meantime there'd be two of us head-on." Keno let a corner of his mouth lift in a wry, not unpleasant smile. "There's her. Make that three."

The Major shook his head promptly. "Not if I stepped out of it. All the way out. Not if I signed over the whole operation—mines, cattle, every-thing—to you."

"What's the string on that?"

"No string. Oh, I'd set aside a piece of money for Luana and that goddam pipsqueak. And keep one of the valley ranches to live out my days on. But for the rest, hell, I'm sixty years old. A man can afford to slack the reins and enjoy what he's built, let a younger man run the whole shebang. Not that you wouldn't be damned glad of the old man's advice when you found what a barrel of headaches you'd taken on. Main thing, it'd be my own blood carrying on. What d'you say?"

Slowly Keno shook his head.

"Why not? What is it?"

"It's different things. For a start, it's you squat-ting on top of this Roost like a fat vulture, feeding off what ain't yours. I ain't throwing no rocks. I done things I ain't nowise proud of. But I never hid under no respectable face while I was doing it, and I never set out to rob them as was dirt poor already."

"Say the word then, boy. Say it and we'll clear off the Roost tomorrow. Leave all this gold for them dumb Utes who'll never live no different anyways. That satisfy you?"

"No."

The Major nodded toward Tally Jo. "The girl? Like Luana said, there's nothing she needs that couldn't be got. Duds, schooling—"

"She's fine like she is." Keno said it flatly. Then moderated his tone. "I don't know if I can make you see how it is. There's a sight more to filling another man's boots than owning up to his blood. I got plans of my own. And the way I am...."

Tally Jo spoke up. "You can understand that, sir. Leastways you ought to."

The Major raised his shaggy brows. "How's that, young lady?"

"Well, sir. I hear tell you come into this valley on shank's mare with naught but a rifle on your shoulder, nigh to forty years ago. And now, why you own just about everything."

"Listen, young lady, there's a difference. My pa left me nothing. I built from scratch. No son of mine needs to."

"No, sir," Tally Jo said firmly. "There ain't one dust mote of difference. Not from one begetting to the next! Not in the feeling a body gets doing for himself."

The Major peered at her sharply. "You had a proper raising, that's clear. Then you know about a boy's duty to his father?"

"Sir, that duty's done. He done it bringing back the money of yours he taken and setting things right with you. That's why he came. But it just don't cut ice, saying what a body should *feel!* Duty and feeling, they's altogether different. A man can force hisself of a duty, like you purse a sickly dog. But there ain't a man alive can feel something that ain't there. And there ain't a solitary reason why he should stay like you want less'n *he* wants to."

The Major sighed heavily. "I stand defeated. All right, boy, tell me about 'em. Your plans..."

Keno did, though reluctantly. The horse and cattle business that had seemed a cinch, backed by the money he would have stolen, had suddenly turned to a hapless dream. His pride began to choke him; he only hoped that Westerman wouldn't ask.

But he did.

"You got the wherewithal to put a footing under that idea, boy?"

Tally Jo, as if to forestall a sharp reply from him, stood up and came over to Keno, standing close and looking up at him solemnly.

"I don't need no favors, Major."

"Goddammit, boy!" Westerman's mouth quivered; his hair bristled. "You can take a wedding gift from your own pa."

"Maybe," Keno said grudgingly, "a loan..."

"All right, goddammit, a loan!" The Major's manner lost its edge. "This girl here—she's worth it, boy, the best start you can give her."

Keno glanced down at Tally Jo in the circle of his arm. "Pa," he said, trying the word, "Pa, there's one thing we don't differ on."

BONNER'S STALLION
T. V. OLSEN

Winner of the Golden Spur Award

Bonner's life is the kind that makes a man hard, makes him love the high country, and makes him fear nothing but being limited by another man's fenceposts. Suddenly it looks as if his life is going to get even harder. He has already lost his woman. Now he is about to lose his son and his mountain ranch to a rich and powerful enemy—a man who hates to see any living thing breathing free. That is when El Diablo Rojo, the feared and hated rogue stallion, comes back into Bonner's life. He and Bonner have one thing in common...they are survivors.

___4276-2 $4.50 US/$5.50 CAN

Dorchester Publishing Co., Inc.
P.O. Box 6640
Wayne, PA 19087-8640

Please add $1.75 for shipping and handling for the first book and $.50 for each book thereafter. NY, NYC, and PA residents, please add appropriate sales tax. No cash, stamps, or C.O.D.s. All orders shipped within 6 weeks via postal service book rate. Canadian orders require $2.00 extra postage and must be paid in U.S. dollars through a U.S. banking facility.

Name_____
Address_____
City_____ State_____ Zip_____
I have enclosed $_____ in payment for the checked book(s).
Payment <u>must</u> accompany all orders. ☐ Please send a free catalog.